A SCORE TO KETTLE

A PEBBLE COVE TEAHOUSE MYSTERY

ERYN SCOTT

Published by Kristopherson Press

www.erynscott.com

erynwrites@gmail.com

Facebook: @erynscottauthor

Sign up for my newsletter to hear about new releases and sales!

Cover by Victoria Cooper

Map by Hanna Sandvig at The Book Cover Bakery

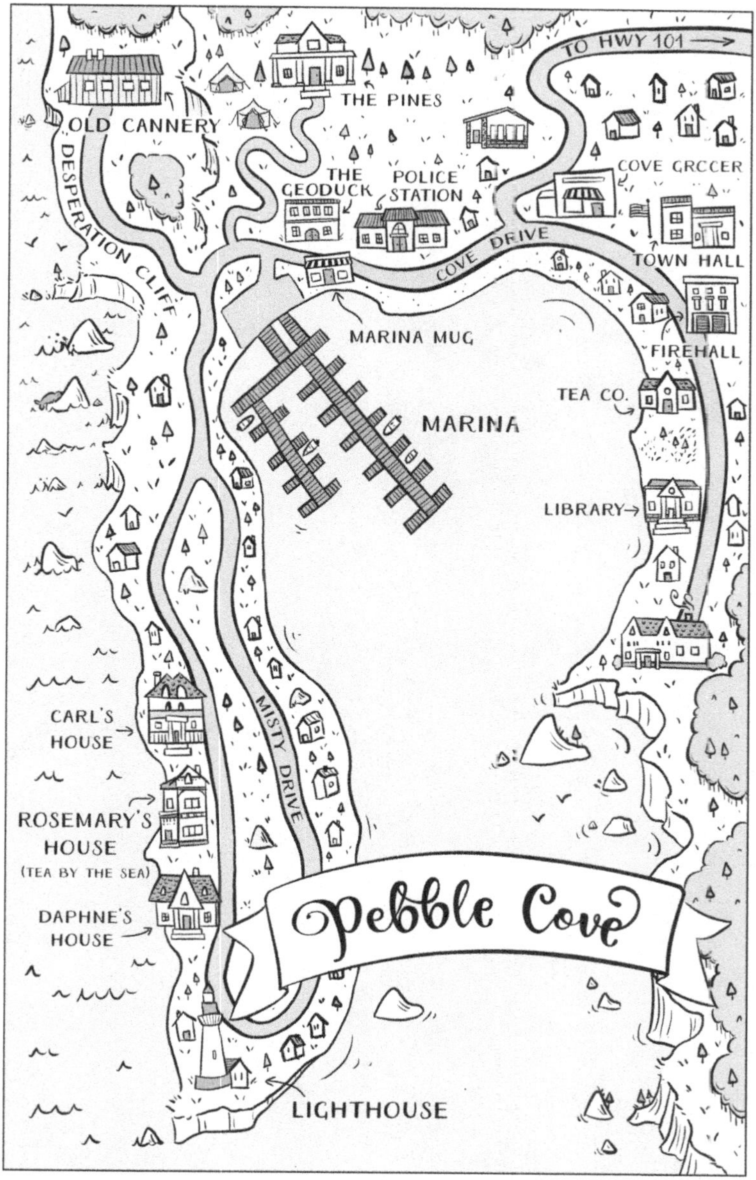
Pebble Cove
TO HWY 101
THE PINES
OLD CANNERY
DESPERATION CLIFF
THE GEODUCK
POLICE STATION
COVE GROCER
TOWN HALL
COVE DRIVE
MARINA MUG
FIREHALL
TEA CO.
MARINA
LIBRARY
MISTY DRIVE
CARL'S HOUSE
ROSEMARY'S HOUSE
(TEA BY THE SEA)
DAPHNE'S HOUSE
LIGHTHOUSE

1

I closed the back door to the tea shop and ran my hands up and down my arms. It was October on the Oregon Coast and a chill rode on the edges of the wind like the whitecaps topping each wave.

Menacing clouds gathered on the horizon. I hoped they stayed away until at least tomorrow. I needed tonight to be clear and perfect for the full moon festival I was catering.

Speaking of tonight, I snatched my list off the table to my right and turned back to my box of supplies. I raked my teeth across my lip as I did a visual check of each item.

Tea. Check.

Electric kettles for boiling. Check.

Cast iron kettles for steeping. Check.

Sugar. Hmmm … I peered into the box, moving items to one side and then the next.

Unable to spot my sugar container, I removed the items from the top of the box and set them on the nearest table.

"I thought you'd already packed all your fancy new catering equipment this morning." Asher entered the room, crossing his arms over his chest and eyeing me. "Why are you taking it all out again?"

"I can't find my sugar," I mumbled as I continued to search. "I don't want to take any chances, Ash. I want tonight to go well." At that moment, I located my sugar jar at the bottom of the box. I glanced back up at him in triumph.

Asher's face softened. "So do I."

He walked toward me, stepping right through a chair on his way forward. It was the kind of ghostly happening that used to make me jump in surprise. But I'd been living with Asher for the better part of seven months and was getting used to it.

He rubbed at his stubbly chin. "Though I would be a lot happier if your first catering job wasn't for *him*." He spat out the last word as if it were a curse. "Did you ask if there will be any howling at the moon?"

Exhaling a laugh, I began repacking the supplies. "No," I said. "I did *not* ask Van whether or not they would be howling. It's a full moon festival, not a werewolf gathering. It'll be painfully hippieish. I bet people will dance, sing-along with a guitar at some point, and maybe lie around on blankets. That's it." I wrinkled my nose, recognizing that most of what I pictured probably came from a documentary on Woodstock my mom and I had watched together a few years back.

"If you're sure," Asher said, his tone dipping low like a warning.

"You're only mad because you can't come with." I turned away from him, grabbing another few bags of tea, just in case.

"No," Asher scoffed. "I'm mad because he swindled you

into doing this. And maybe a little because it's at The Pines."

I pressed my lips together so I wouldn't pick a fight. It wasn't Asher's fault he was sour about that place; the house on the hill held awful memories for both of us. Me because I'd had a scary, near-death experience there earlier this year, and Asher because authorities had discovered his body in the woods surrounding the farmhouse.

While the place had sat vacant for a few months after being rented out to a particularly awful woman—and one who now sat in prison for double homicide—the rightful owner had passed away a few months ago, leaving the home and surrounding acreage to his son.

The family had owned the property for over a hundred years. And while the townspeople of Pebble Cove were happy to have someone from the Mills family back in the house, Asher didn't share their excitement.

It didn't help that the man who'd moved in was named Sullivan Mills. Even though he went by Van—and was three generations removed from his great-grandfather, and namesake—one would think Asher was back in the early 1900s, dealing with his self-proclaimed nemesis, Sullivan Mills the first.

"Van is different from the rest of his family. He's not crazy about money like them. He's opened a peaceful living community, for Pete's sake," I said defensively. "Plus, I thought you'd like him since he's the reason we know the truth about how you died."

Asher huffed. Until a few months ago, we'd been under the unfortunate impression that Asher had taken his own life after deserting his post as an officer in the army during World War I. But Van's renovation of the property—taking down trees to allow for more yurts for his community members—had uncovered a skeleton. Asher's skeleton. And with the bones came the undeniable proof that someone had hit him over the head from behind.

He hadn't deserted his post after all. Someone made sure he couldn't show up for his unit's deployment.

Looking over my list one last time, I felt like maybe I was ready. A good thing too. It was past six-thirty, and the sun was disappearing below the sea. The sky would be inky and the moon visible in an hour when the festival began.

I continued my argument. "Without Van Mills, we wouldn't know the truth about you. Shouldn't that make him your favorite Mills by far?"

I surveyed my catering equipment, another thing we wouldn't have without Van Mills.

During his first visit to Tea by the Sea a few months back, my grandmother's tea blends had floored the man. He'd insisted I cater his upcoming full moon festival, the event he was holding to commemorate the first full month of The Pines: A Sustainable Community being open. While Van had tried floating other names around town, the locals were so used to calling it The Pines that I guess Van figured, why fight it?

When I'd turned Van's business offer down, citing my lack of mobile equipment as the reason, he'd offered to purchase more electric hot-water kettles, durable tea kettles for steeping, and mugs so I wouldn't have to worry about breaking my grandmother's supply of clay and porcelain tea sets.

Realizing he had never answered my question about Van, I eyed Asher. He set his ghostly jaw in defiance.

"He'd be my favorite if I wasn't sure he has ulterior motives for asking you up to his commune tonight." Asher narrowed his eyes in the direction of the hill that housed the large farmhouse and newly erected yurt village.

"Community," I corrected. "Van says the word commune has too heavy a connotation. It's a community." I ignored Asher's comment about Van's motivation.

I couldn't deny that the man had flirted with me every time he'd come into the tea shop. From touching my hand whenever he could, to complimenting my long hair, I couldn't help but wonder if tea was all he was after.

"Plus," I said, "if I get into trouble I can use one of these cast-iron tea kettles as a weapon." I picked one of the heavy pots out of the box and swung it playfully.

Asher smiled for the first time since he'd entered the room.

"But I won't need to hit anyone over the head with a kettle. Jolene will be with me. She'll make sure I'm safe," I said.

Asher nodded as if that was the only consolation in this whole terrible scenario.

My business partner and friend would bring her own contribution to the full moon festival tonight. I'd tried one of her homemade moon pies and couldn't wait to sample one of the delicate chamomile cakes she'd created for tonight's festivities.

In the months since I'd begun working with her, Jolene and I had not only grown close, but our collaboration had also doubled our previous monthly profits.

Asher moved toward the window as I checked the boxes for the last few things on my list. His broad shoulders sank, and I tried to remember he wasn't being difficult for nothing. The man had been through a lot—both in his life and afterlife.

"Look," I said, "I promise I'll tell you every detail when

I come back tonight, safe and sound. I'm sure I'll have funny stories about quirky yurt people and something concrete to add to the *Van's actually a nice guy* list I'm making to convince you."

Asher turned toward me. His face was set in disbelief, but there was a smile hiding behind those familiar blue eyes. I caught myself again—as I often did—forgetting he wasn't real. His spirit was at its strongest here at his old house, so he appeared as real as anyone alive did to me. But if I reached out to touch him, my hand would waft right through.

I busied myself by tucking a few last-minute napkins into my catering supplies, not sure the stack I'd already packed would be enough. "I'm sure Van will show you how much the Mills family has changed over the years. Just because you didn't get along with his great-grandfather doesn't mean there's something wrong with their genetics."

When I glanced back at Asher, the lightness in his eyes had been surpassed by darkness, like a troubling cloud rolling in over stormy seas.

I was about to ask what that expression was about when the bells on the tea shop's front door jangled, signaling a forced end to our conversation. Jolene must be here. While I'd shared a lot about myself and my past with my friend and business partner, I'd yet to tell anyone about my ability to see and talk to ghosts.

"Well then," Asher said, running a hand through his almost black hair. "I'll make myself scarce. Be safe, Rosemary."

I mouthed a quick "thank you" to him. Asher knew that I had the tendency to slip and look at or talk to him regardless of who was in the room, forgetting that I was the only one who could see and hear him. Sometimes he removed himself so I wouldn't be tempted.

"Hello," Jolene trilled out as she entered. "You ready?" she asked as she reached the end of the entry hallway and laid eyes on me.

Her curly black hair was streaked with silver in such a beautiful way that it almost seemed like she'd colored it that way on purpose. She'd pulled her hair into a large clip today and wore a long skirt, a tie-dyed cardigan, and about six colorful scarves.

"You'll fit right in." I chuckled.

Jolene spun to give me the full effect. "When in a commune."

"Community," we both corrected at the same time, then followed it with a laugh.

"Maybe I should change." I glanced down at my jeans, boots, and wool sweater.

Jolene waved her hand. "You'll be fine. Word around town is that they're a bunch of rich yuppies, not real hippies."

"That's the Rickster," I scoffed. "He droned on for ten minutes about 'what a shame' it was when I ran into him downtown yesterday."

Though the community had officially been open for a month now, they didn't venture into town often, and Jolene and I were the first locals Van had invited up to the property.

"It's not only the Rickster who's upset." Jolene's eyes widened. "Everyone's up in arms about this entire thing. Apparently, Van assured the town council there would only be a dozen guests staying on the property, but a few made a stop at Cove Grocer yesterday, and it sounds like there's at least double that."

I was glad I'd packed extra supplies.

"I made a double batch of both my recipes after hearing that," Jolene said. "Besides being upset about the number of guests, the town's already complaining about the place in general. A few people were up in arms that the community members were coming into town, while others were worried that they haven't come into town more. Some are mad because they think the community members will all be naked; others are mad because they *don't* think they'll be naked. Well, that last one is mostly the Rickster."

Cringing, I said, "Do you think we should still do this? I don't want the town to be mad at us for working there and stop coming to our shops."

Jolene laughed. "Mad and curious are not mutually exclusive emotions. They need someone to infiltrate and report back, and we're the first ones to be invited. After tonight, both our shops will be packed with locals."

"Okay," I said, clapping my hands together. "Then let's do this."

Jolene helped me carry my supplies out to her car. I eyed the murky cloud in the dimming light, but the storm seemed like it was still too far out to sea to be much of a threat tonight. Even so, it felt like an ominous warning sitting on the horizon. Or maybe it was Asher's concern for my safety that sat like a pit in my stomach.

Little did I know, I wasn't the one who would be in mortal danger that night.

2

Jolene's SUV wended its way up the road, climbing up the hill toward The Pines. A chill coated my skin like a cold sweat. I hadn't been to visit the white farmhouse on the hill since I'd almost died there—well, had almost been killed was more like it.

I held my breath in anticipation as we rounded the last bend. The rush of fear I expected to hit me as the place came into view didn't manifest. I felt shocked, sure, but not frightened.

The barn where I'd been tied up had been removed, for one thing. It wasn't the only thing missing either. They had removed trees all around the property, opening up the space considerably.

Someone had strung delicate, warm fairy lights in each of the gnarled fruit trees lining the last bit of the driveway as we approached the house. In the extensive field behind the trees sat about twenty circular linen yurt tents, the kind you might see pictured in an article about "glamping." Each reminded me of a large, fabric version of a paper lantern, and I half expected them to lift off the grass and float away as we drove by.

Last time I'd been here, there had only been a half-dozen cars in the parking spots next to the house. With the barn gone, there was more space, and gleaming luxury vehicles filled each available spot.

Between the number of cars and the field full of tents, it appeared the hubbub in town about extra people had been warranted. There were definitely more than a dozen people here tonight. Jolene almost couldn't find a spot to park, but spotted a small opening next to a shiny black Mercedes.

Stepping out of her modest SUV, we eyed the expensive vehicles. We agreed to find Van before attempting to unpack any of our supplies. Jolene and I gave each other a fortifying glance before walking down the brick pathway, toward the sounds of chatter, music, and laughter.

The air was cool but pleasant and smelled of sweet pine boughs and mowed grass. Every once in a while, a chill would skirt past, rushing through my sweater and swiping icy fingers at my skin. Any residual light from the setting sun had faded, and the full moon was now visible in the indigo sky above. Our shoes sank into the cool grass as we left the pathway and headed toward the center of the field where most of the people congregated.

Now that we closed in on the crowd, I noticed I'd been completely wrong about how they would be dressed. There wasn't a hint of tie-dye in sight nor a whisper of fringe. This wasn't a Woodstock-esque gathering at all. It looked more like an REI store had exploded. Arc'teryx jackets, North Face fleeces, GORE-TEX windbreakers, and every other top-end outdoor brand seemed to be accounted for.

Jolene and I set course for the main meeting area, a place that had large ornate rugs laid onto the cool grass and tables set up along the edge. But before we even reached the area, a man approached us. He had the athletic build of a swimmer and the light brown curls of a surfer. He also had the countenance of a winter storm blowing into shore.

"Excuse us," I reached out with a timid voice. "Could you point us in the direction of Van? We're the caterers, and we need to check in with him."

The man's face, which was already pulled into a grimace, creased even more as he spit out his response. "I don't know where that slimeball is, but if I find him first, it won't matter because he'll be a dead man."

I gulped. Already on edge about being here, the last thing I needed was mention of death. Without so much as an explanation or apology, the man continued his stomping and traveled past us, up toward the main farmhouse.

Jolene turned to me and frowned. "Friendly welcome."

"Right? I wonder what that was all about."

"Don't worry about Cinder; he's got a bit of a temper." A woman's voice came from behind us.

Understandably jumpy after that encounter, Jolene and I gasped and spun around. A woman stood a couple of yards away, her hands on tweed pantsuit-clad hips. Her brunette hair was styled into a bob. She looked to be about my age—mid-twenties—but the confidence with which she held herself and her high-powered business exterior made me wonder if my guess was too low.

Although her outfit screamed money, like the rest of the people here, her businesswoman appearance directly contrasted their outdoor adventurer aesthetic. The expensive kitten heels she wore sank into the damp grass.

She glanced back to where Cinder had disappeared and snorted. "Not sure what my brother did to make him mad this time, but he'll cool down. You two must be the caterers," she said, turning back to us.

We held out our hands to shake hers as we introduced ourselves.

"Good to meet you. I'm Liv Mills, Van's sister." She motioned at the dirt road skirting the lawn. "If you want to drive your car down this way, you could unload your supplies here, which will be way closer."

"That would be great." I eyed the distance, liking the idea of a few hundred feet better than the five-minute walk it would've been to and from the parking lot.

Jolene pulled out her keys. "I'll go get the car if you want to check out the setup," she said to me.

I nodded. Liv walked with me toward the tables as Jolene went off toward the car.

"I didn't realize Van had a sister," I said conversationally.

Liv snorted. "Really? I figured this town would've had a file a couple of inches thick on our family by now."

Eyebrows lifting with interest, I said, "Well, I'm new to town, sort of. So I'm still learning about the history."

I didn't let on that I'd felt more at home in Pebble Cove than anywhere else I'd ever been, or that I already knew about the Mills family, hoping she'd try to fill in some blanks for me.

"That's good," Liv said, studying me for a moment. "Now I don't have to worry that you have a bunch of opinions about us already."

Before I could ask her what that meant, her brother approached wearing a charming half smile. His brown hair was swept off to one side, mirrored by his mouth, which tugged up in only one corner.

Van was clean cut in that way that only comes with

growing up rich. His clothes looked new. His tan was perfect, like he had cultivated it on yachts and beaches instead of working outside. And even though he was wearing a fleece zip up and jeans, closer examination proved they were from brand names I'd probably never be able to afford.

I shook the negative thoughts from my mind. Van had mentioned how he was trying to be different from his money-hungry father. The whole point behind the community he built here was to give people a way to connect and center themselves. He wanted to give back.

"My favorite tea shop owner." Van opened his arms wide and pulled me into a hug.

Heat practically emanated off his body, though he wasn't sweaty. He'd probably been running around, trying to get everything ready for tonight. Shivering a little as I pulled away from him, I hoped the movement of unpacking would warm me up.

"I see you met my sister." He turned his grin toward Liv.

"Yes." I gestured to her and the tables. "Liv was showing me where to put our supplies."

Moving past my comment, Liv turned to her brother and said, "Cinder is looking for you too."

Van's smile dropped, free falling for a second before he caught it. "Perfect, I'll go find him." Cool and calm again, he turned to me. "Will you be okay setting up for a few, on your own?"

I assured him I would and noticed Jolene pulling her car down the dirt road. Liv watched her brother leave, concern written on the creases in her face and evident in the length of time she stared after him.

Pausing before going to help Jolene, I said, "Is everything okay?"

Liv blinked as if she'd forgotten I was there. "Yeah, sorry. Just a big sister worrying about my little brother. It's what I do best." She waved a hand at me. "If you're okay, I'll catch up with you later."

As I had with Van, I told her we would be fine. Liv left in an equally odd manner. I went to help Jolene.

It didn't take us long to unpack and have the tables ready. Between Jolene's beautiful, perfect chamomile cakes—complete with a yellow and white flower on top—and her decadent moon pies, I couldn't wait to see everyone's reactions. People had been milling around while we'd worked, and they seemed as impressed as I was with Jolene's desserts.

For my part, I had almost all the kettles full of boiling water, steeping unique blends. I'd brought the largest amount of my chamomile blend, as that was the one Van had liked best when he'd visited.

"Should I make one more pot of the chamomile blend?" I wondered aloud, glancing toward Jolene to see what she thought.

She peered into the box I'd brought. "I don't think you can. You're out of teapots."

I counted in my head as I passed by the others sitting on the table. "That's weird, I should have twelve." I only counted eleven on the table. Maybe I'd left one back at the tea shop with all of my packing and unpacking. Shrugging, I said, "Think we can let them start?" I checked my watch. It was past eight, and the sky was pitch black. The full moon hung above us like a shimmering silver coin.

Jolene looked around. "Wasn't Van going to come back and tell us what to do next?"

"I thought he was, but it's getting late. He said they would start at eight, so I guess we wait," I said, scanning the people mingling on the lawn.

There had to be two dozen people now as more had emerged from their yurts. Even though they weren't wearing tie-dye, they lounged around on expensive-looking carpets, playing instruments, and picking flowers. Not a one of them was naked; however, I'd have to let the Rickster know that much.

A few minutes later, one of the community members came over and told us Van had texted her to say we could start serving. I wondered where he was, where he'd disappeared to. The man didn't strike me as the hands-off kind with this community. I'd expected he would be here, in the middle of the festival. Worry crept up my throat as I wondered if he and Cinder had found each other. Judging by how angry Cinder had been, I didn't predict that meeting would end well for Van.

But he'd texted someone. That meant he had to be okay. The two of them were probably somewhere talking through their issue in a calm manner befitting two people who were part of a peaceful-living community.

I tried to loosen the tension in my shoulders by rolling them back and focusing on tea service. Doing a quick pour from each of my kettles, I double-checked that I had steeped each one to perfection. Community members crowded around, eyes sparkling with the combination of fairy lights and full moon shimmer as they took in our refreshments.

But before any of the guests could so much as grab a moon pie or pour a cup of tea, a young woman came rushing toward the festivities, tears streaming down her face, a strangled scream caught in her throat.

"What's wrong?" a man asked her. He caught her arms and gripped tight as if he worried she wouldn't stop running if he didn't block her.

"It's Clover," she coughed the words out in a sob. "She's dead."

Stomach dropping, I couldn't tell if we all went pale or if it was merely the full moon bathing us in the same silvery light. The group of us ran after the woman as she led us to one of the cozy, inviting yurts. The door flaps were open, tied back like curtains, and gave us a straight view into the tented living space.

Inside, the scene wasn't cozy at all. A woman about my age lay sprawled on a rug similar to the ones laid out in the festival area. She was dressed in jeans, boots, and a warm sweater, like me. Her blonde hair was matted with blood. A large object sat next to her head, obviously the murder weapon as it held a mirrored patch of blood.

I swallowed the bile rising in my throat and looked at Jolene as I saw her attention settle on the murder weapon.

I'd found my missing cast-iron tea kettle.

3

A half hour later, I pulled the sleeves of my sweater over my hands and tucked them under my armpits to keep them warm. While the storm cloud had stayed away, the night had brought with it a different kind of chill.

Death.

Liv had left to go find her brother, leaving us to stand among the rest of the festival onlookers. Police Chief Clemenson had arrived a few minutes prior. He scowled as he jotted down details in his notebook. Jolene and I stood a couple of yards away from where he questioned the person who'd found the body.

And while Jolene and the other festival-goers traded theories and statements of disbelief, I listened in on the chief's conversation.

"So you said it was just after eight when you found her?" he asked.

"Yes, w-we were s-supposed to go to the festival together," stammered the young woman I'd learned was named Meadow. Her fingers shook as she raked them through her brunette ponytail.

Meadow and the chief turned to peer inside the yurt at Clover's body. The flaps were still open, but there was a line of yellow police tape preventing anyone from entering. Inside, Officer Kennedy documented the crime scene with Dr. Ellis. Meadow broke into a new fit of sobs. The seasoned police chief swallowed and focused on rereading his notes.

"When was the last time you saw her before that?" he asked, handing Meadow a tissue.

She blew her nose. "We had dinner together around six, but then we split up to get changed and stuff before the festival. But that's definitely the last time I saw her. I swear."

My ears perked up at the last part of her statement. *I swear.* It sounded defensive. I studied Meadow's face, taking in her pinched expression and shifty eyes. I would bet money that was a lie. Luckily, the chief caught the same signs. I'd seen his face enough times when he thought I was lying and recognized the combination of a sigh and the tensing of his jaw.

"Oh, wow. Chief, you gotta come see this," Officer Kennedy called out from the crime scene.

At that exclamation, all the people gathered around turned their attention toward the yurt, and I was no longer the only one listening in. Chief Clemenson shook his head almost imperceptibly in frustration, but from the way Kennedy flinched as he watched his boss approach, I'd say he caught the nonverbal reprimand.

Dr. Ellis crouched next to the body, next to Clover's hand. Kennedy peered down at the hand. The chief joined his officer, craning his neck in the same way. I couldn't tell what was in her hand, but whatever it was had to be shocking from the way the chief's features lit up in surprise.

Frown lines deepening on his face, Clemenson returned

to Meadow. This time he spoke in a much lower tone, facing away from me, so I couldn't hear what he asked her.

Meadow's head shot back at the question. She blinked for a moment, then shook her head fervently.

The chief marked something in his notebook before calling Kennedy over. The officer walked away with Meadow, presumably taking her back to her yurt. From the pallor her face adopted before leaving, I was sure the chief had given her his usual warning of, "Don't leave town. I'm going to have more questions for you."

The chief flipped through his notes. Seeing my chance, I broke away from the group and jogged over to him.

He said nothing, but cocked an eyebrow at me.

"I don't know if Meadow mentioned this, so I just thought you should know," I said, pointing into the yurt, "that's my cast-iron kettle."

Chief Clemenson's features remained steady, but he tipped his head ever so slightly to one side in an "oh, really?" way.

Face heating, I stammered, "Uh—I mean—that's not to say … I didn't hit her with it." My shoulders slumped in my disappointment with myself. "Someone took it from my catering set."

His eyebrows rose this time. "And you witnessed them take it?"

Clearing my throat, I said, "Well, no. But I realized it was missing right before Meadow came running to tell us about Clover. We were about to start service at that point." I gestured over to Jolene, hoping the reminder I worked with someone he liked better than me would help with his mood. "Which means she had to have been hit in the last hour."

The chief let his head move to the other side now. "Let me get this straight, Miss Woodmere …"

My already fiery face burned even more as I realized I'd said something wrong, or maybe all the things wrong, considering the length of the pause he took.

"Someone took one of your tea kettles right from under your nose, while you set up, and yet you have no idea who could've done such a thing?" His tone was drier than the toast I'd accidentally burnt that morning for my breakfast.

Cringing, I felt like Lucy Ricardo making her iconic "I'm in trouble face" after Ricky caught her in one of her harebrained schemes.

"I guess so," I said in a croaky whisper. "I thought it might help with time of death."

What was I saying? Why was I saying this? Who did I think I was, a detective? Well, I had helped solve the last few murders in this town, so maybe shouldn't doubt myself. The chief, however, didn't seem to share my feelings.

"Thank you, I'm sure Dr. Ellis would've been lost without that clue." He scribbled something into his notebook.

I wished Asher were here to read over his shoulder and tell me what he was writing. Knowing the chief, it was probably something about how I was acting shifty and should be considered a suspect even though this was the first time in my life I'd ever seen this woman.

"You're also telling me that's why your fingerprints will be on that kettle right there?" the chief continued his questioning, making my blunder sound even worse and even more nefarious.

I'd come over here to be helpful and now sounded more and more like a killer covering my tracks.

"Chief, I swear, I've never seen that woman before in my life." I pointed to the body in the yurt.

He leveled a stare at me, the same tight-jawed one he'd

directed at Meadow. I realized too late that I'd sounded as suspicious and guilty as Meadow had, insisting she hadn't seen Clover since right after dinner. Maybe Meadow wasn't lying after all; maybe the chief flustered people.

Waving, I backed away. "Okay, I'll be over here if you need anything."

The chief didn't stop me as I moved toward Jolene and the group of onlookers.

"What'd he have to say?" Jolene asked as I returned.

Groaning, I said, "Not much. He didn't need to because I babbled the entire time and made myself seem guilty."

Even in the darkness, Jolene's confusion was easy enough to spot. "Guilty of what?"

"I don't know." I sighed. "Somehow being responsible for that poor girl in there being hit with one of my teapots."

Jolene chuckled but then stopped herself as she seemed to realize the situation was too serious for laughter. "The chief doesn't consider you a suspect. Trust me. I can be your alibi since I've been with you for the whole night."

My lips tipped up. "Thanks. You didn't notice anyone hanging around our boxes of stuff, did you?" I asked. "I can't figure out how someone got one of my teapots while we stood right there."

"I've been wondering the same thing." Jolene scratched at the side of her nose. "There were a lot of people hanging around and watching us work, so it's not out of the question. But one of us would've noticed if someone walked away with one of your new treasures."

I agreed. "And your car was locked when we went to find Van when we first got here?"

Jolene inhaled sharply. "I left it unlocked. Omigosh, do you think the killer went into my car and stole the kettle?"

"I'm afraid that's exactly what happened."

My friend's shoulders sank.

"You couldn't have known." I patted her on the back.

"That means someone killed her while we set up." Jolene shook her shoulders as if it might remove the creepiness.

Reminded of our tea and treats, I said, "Should we still serve everything?" Even though it had been awhile, I'd tested the cast-iron kettles, and they kept stuff fairly warm for a long time. I might have to add a little more boiling water, but it would be better than nothing.

"You know, that might be a nice distraction." Jolene nodded and headed over to the crime scene. "Let me go tell the chief."

Jolene gestured over toward our catering tables once the chief turned to greet her. My gaze followed. The tables and lights looked like a peaceful party, a scene from a completely different night. The chief smiled in response, and I wished I'd been the one to go tell him. I needed all the extra points with him I could get.

"He says that sounds like an outstanding idea," Jolene told me before calling the rest of the community members over to our tables for tea and desserts.

The people followed us like little ducklings, still somber but spirits obviously raised by the promise of food—if their chatter was any indication.

Five minutes later, we stood around the tables, talking to the community members while they sipped and ate. The majority of the crying had ceased with the introduction of food, but fear still settled over the group like a low cloud. Even though the police were only a few hundred feet away, there was still a killer on the loose, possibly even among us. I studied the people surrounding the tables.

"I can't believe she's gone," a woman said after taking a bite of chamomile cake.

The woman she stood next to shook her head, long curls bouncing back and forth with the motion. "I know, and to think anyone could've been upset with her or dislike her enough to do anything like this. That's the most unbelievable thing."

"What was she like?" I asked, unable to help myself.

"She was so kind," a third woman said. This one wore a thick headband holding her golden hair back from her face. "And, like, how she lived her life so mindfully and tech free was such an inspiration to me." Tears fell down her cheek, and she sniffed.

"I'd hate to be the one who has to tell Cinder," a woman with curly hair said, checking over her shoulder as if the angry man I'd met earlier might be standing behind her.

I turned to her and asked, "Why?"

The curly-haired woman blinked in the moonlight. "He and Clover were together."

My stomach dropped. The dead woman was in a relationship with the hothead we'd met earlier? My mind flicked through the possibilities like fingers searching through a box of recipes.

But he'd been mad at Van. Cinder had said nothing about Clover.

"When was the last time anyone saw him?" I asked the group, feeling a lot like the chief with this line of questioning.

Each person looked at someone else as if they didn't want to be the one to say it. Finally, a skinny young man raised his hand as if he were still in high school. Between his baby face and innocent demeanor, maybe he was.

"He stormed past me around seven." The kid flinched, glancing over his shoulder.

That checked out. That had been right when Jolene and

I encountered him storming toward the house. *Toward the parking lot*, the thought clicked in my mind. Toward Jolene's unlocked car with the kettle inside. That gave him opportunity and means. But what about motive?

The young man's mention of Cinder's tantrum seemed to jog another person's memory because the woman with long curls sucked in a breath. "I overheard an argument between him and Clover in her yurt after dinner. I mean, I couldn't make out what they said, just that they were both upset. Do you think …?" She didn't finish the question.

She didn't have to.

Cinder could've had a fight with Clover earlier, then stewed and did something about it once he saw the kettles sitting in Jolene's car as he stormed past. It would've been the perfect opportunity since most of the community members were in the gathering area at that point instead of in their yurts.

"You two need to go tell all of this to Chief Clemenson," I said, gesturing toward the crime scene where the chief spoke with Dr. Ellis.

As if he read my mind, the chief chose that moment to walk over to us. "I'm Pebble Cove's police chief. Thank you for sticking around. I'll need to question each person who lives here on the compound, one by one."

I cringed, knowing Van would've hated the use of the word compound. It was another of those words "with a lot of baggage" he'd explained when I'd asked him why he was staying away from commune and compound.

Clemenson turned to Jolene. "Jo, you and Rosemary can clean up and get out of here. I'll come talk to you tomorrow. I've already gotten Miss Woodmere's take on the situation." He said the last part like my *take* on it was all wrong.

The cakes and moon pies had gone fast—apparently

tragedy made people hungry—and they'd already sipped the last drop of my tea, so I was happy to leave. The sigh that leaked out of me as we turned to clean up was more representative of the feeling I'd taken two giant leaps back in my relationship with the chief.

The crowd followed him as he led them over to the farmhouse for questioning. I turned back to our tables, pulling out my boxes to pack.

"Don't take him too seriously. He means well," Jolene said.

I glanced up at the full moon, thinking about the festival that didn't matter anymore. Instead, we'd catered a crime scene, becoming a necessary comfort rather than a celebration.

"I know," I conceded. "At least this seems like a cut-and-dried case. Sounds like that guy Cinder we met earlier is the culprit here."

Jolene packed away her platters while I readied my teapots for travel. "I hope the chief wraps this up quickly. I don't like the thought of a killer in our town again."

That same clammy feeling returned, and fear pricked at the back of my neck. I agreed. The two of us packed up our supplies as promptly as we could. I was more than ready to leave The Pines behind me.

4

"I told you it was an awful idea for you to go tonight," Asher said when Jolene dropped me off at the tea shop thirty minutes later.

I held a heavy box of catering supplies, so I did something I generally avoided and walked straight through him into the tearoom.

"How'd you hear?" I asked flatly. I was exhausted, cold, and freaked out.

"Tim heard Kennedy's radio when he got the call. Officer K was on the boardwalk trying to coax that raccoon out of under the bridge again, and you know how Tim gets a kick out of watching him struggle. Tim told Max, who told Lois, who told me." Asher folded his arms in front of his chest, eyeing me.

Right. The ghost rumor mill in this town worked faster than the regular one.

"Oh, come on," I said. "There's no way you could've known something like this would happen. Plus, it didn't happen to me. It barely had anything to do with me." I cocked an eyebrow at him as I set the box down.

"Barely?" he asked, moving closer. "That means it did a little?"

Wrinkling my nose, I said, "Well, you know how I mentioned using those cast-iron kettles as a weapon?" I grimaced. "It turns out, I wasn't the only one with that idea."

Asher's expression mirrored mine. "Ouch. So you're involved because someone used one of your kettles to kill the poor woman?"

I reluctantly nodded.

Asher shot me a sidelong glance. "Now that we know those things can be used as weapons, you need to keep a better eye on where you put them."

"Ha ha," I said dryly, but then tipped my head in question. "Why do I need to be more careful?" I asked, wondering how he knew about us leaving them unlocked in Jolene's car.

"You left one behind with all your packing and unpacking." Asher motioned to the table in the tearoom where I'd been working earlier that evening.

My fatigue forgotten, I whipped around to see he was right. There, sitting innocently on the table, was my twelfth cast-iron kettle.

"Which means it wasn't mine at all," I muttered to myself.

"What?" Asher moved closer to me.

Pressing my eyes closed for a second so I could think this through, I said, "I lost a tea kettle and then one showed up at the crime scene. I figured it was mine. But if my missing kettle was here the whole time …" My eyes flashed open. "Oh no. I may have misled the chief about the victim's time of death. And now there's a second mystery to solve: where the killer got a teapot exactly like the ones I have."

Asher scoffed, "That's not a mystery at all. Look to the source." When I gave him a questioning glare, he added, "Who bought the things for you in the first place? Whose property were you on tonight?"

"You think Van had something to do with this?" I was about to shake my head and explain that Van had been missing most of the night, when I realized how that sounded. "Oh …" was the only thing I could think to say.

Outside the large picture windows of the tea shop, the full moon glittered off the surface of the waves. That same storm cloud sat looming on the horizon. In the night sky, I couldn't tell if it was any closer or if it had moved away from us.

"I wish you'd been able to come tonight." I turned my attention back to Asher. "It would've been nice to see what the chief had been writing in his notebook. Oh, and what the mysterious thing was the victim had clutched in her hand."

"Hold on, Lois only told me a young woman was killed at the commune. I don't know any details other than what you told me about the murder weapon. Care to fill me in?" Asher gestured to the library, where we spent most nights reading and talking.

Still chilled to the bone, nothing sounded better than sinking into my favorite couch with a wool blanket draped over my shoulders. I led the way to my favorite room in the house.

Asher listened with the same focus and intensity he always did, nodding and adopting ponderous expressions as I went through the events of the night. But when I described the clues proving Cinder had to be the one who killed Clover, Asher didn't look so convinced.

But he hadn't met the guy. After seeing how worked up

the man had been when we'd arrived, it didn't seem like a stretch at all to picture him losing all control and hurting someone, especially the person he'd been arguing with earlier that evening.

Asher crossed his arms. "I still think Van's to blame. It's got to be him."

I sighed. "Why? What makes you think that?"

"I don't know, Rosemary," he said pointedly. "I simply feel it in my bones."

We both contemplated that statement. Asher didn't have bones, or a body.

He smiled. "You know what I mean."

"A gut feeling." I nodded, then we laughed again. Asher didn't have guts either. But my good mood soured as I thought about Asher putting the blame on Van. "Just because you hated his great-grandfather, doesn't mean Van is a bad person, and definitely doesn't mean he's a murderer."

The wind picked up outside, pushing against the plants in the garden outside the library window, causing their branches to squeak and tap against the glass.

"Hey," I said, realizing something. "If The Pines is Sully's old house, and you were killed there, why can't you travel there now?"

Asher could only manifest as a ghostly body in places he'd set foot when he was alive. He was the strongest in places he spent the most time, but became transparent—more traditionally ghostlike—when we ventured to areas he'd frequented less during his life.

"First of all, the house that's standing there now is *quite* different from the place Sully lived in back when I was alive," Asher said.

I remembered him explaining that part of the reason

Abigail still planned to marry Asher instead of the man she loved, Sullivan Mills, was because of money. Meaning, Asher's family had it, Sully's didn't. The stately white farmhouse that sat in the center of The Pines' property today gave my Victorian beach house a run for its grandeur and definitely didn't fit the picture of a poor family.

"The closest I ever got were those woods surrounding the house," Asher said. "In fact, right by the place they dug up my body was where my friend Jimmy and I used to hide and mess with Sully." A playful smirk tugged up one corner of Asher's mouth.

"Hide and seek?" I asked, finding his grin contagious.

"Not exactly. There was this big stump from a tree that must've been hit by lightning at some point. It's not easy to see, but the stump is hollow, and if you walked around it clockwise, you could slip through the small opening and hide inside. We might've learned from some other boys in our class that Sully had a terrible fear of coyotes, so we sat in that trunk and made coyote sounds when Sully was supposed to be out doing his chores for the evening." Asher chuckled, still enjoying the prank a century later.

Snorting, I said, "Gee, I wonder why you and Sully never got along."

Asher's happy expression vanished. "He started it. I wouldn't have done anything if he hadn't—"

A flash of lightning over the ocean interrupted him, stealing our focus for a moment. I counted in my head, straining to hear for the following thunder, hoping to gauge how far away the strike had been. I got to nine before a distant rumble sounded. My shoulders relaxed, and I leaned back into the couch.

Asher did the same and met my gaze as he turned away from the window.

"Sorry, you were saying." I gestured for him to continue.

While his expression had changed to that of interest and anticipation with the lightning, my mention of his Sully story brought his face back to that stormy version.

"Sully didn't merely hate me from the moment we met; I'm convinced he'd been cultivating those feelings long before we'd been introduced. Which meant he loathed me completely by the time we came face-to-face in school." Asher's tone held an acidic sting at the edges.

"How would he have learned to hate you before he even met you?" I asked, feeling exhausted like I was being pulled into someone else's friendship drama.

"His father hated my family. He hated that my father had created a successful company. He hated that he worked for him, that he made less than him, that he had to take orders from him, and he really hated it when my father fired him for insubordination." Asher's jaw jutted forward. "While the Benson family name was commonplace at their dinner table, I'm sure not a word of it was complimentary. Which meant when Sully and I met at school for the first time, he punched me, breaking my nose, and calling my father all sorts of deplorable names."

I leaned forward. "The very first time you met him? How old were you?"

"Six."

I lifted a hand to my mouth. "I'm so sorry. I can't even imagine six-year-olds fighting, let alone him breaking your nose."

Asher's lips peeled up into a self-satisfied grin. "Don't worry, that was the last time he caught me unaware. I got him back many times over."

I rolled my eyes, not understanding the need for violence or rivalry. "So I'm guessing his father never forgave your father? I would've thought they'd moved past it since the family obviously made a lot of money eventually."

"Sully and Abigail's son, Sullivan Junior, or SJ, was the one who made the money in the family, but he didn't make a cent of it until he was an adult with his own children. Sully and Abigail were both long gone. They died in their forties, a couple years apart, of completely treatable conditions." Asher shook his head.

"That's awful," I said, pulling my blanket tighter around me.

"Well, their deaths were brought on by an insurmountable level of stubbornness and narrow-sighted bullheadedness." Asher's tone sharpened again.

I sighed. "Okay, but if SJ could pull the whole family out of poverty and make a big enough fortune that his grandson inherited enough to build a sustainable living community on the old family property, that should show you that people can change. Neither Van nor any of the Mills family members are killers."

"Rosemary," Asher said seriously, "my body was found at the edge of Sullivan's property. It's not that I just didn't get along with the man. The more I think about it, the more I'm sure Sully's the person who killed me."

5

The library pulsed and spun around me after Asher's statement. It was too late in the night for revelations like this.

"Killed you? Why would Sully kill you?" And even as I asked, I knew the answer.

Abigail.

Asher's fiancée seemed to get on my nerves even in the afterlife, as if she were here in ghostly form too.

Miss Abigail Glaser had been set to marry Asher when he returned from war even though she no longer loved him. In fact, she'd fallen in love with another man, none other than Asher's least favorite person, Sullivan Mills.

"He killed you to get you out of the way?" I asked. "But you were going to war. Why not bank on you dying during the war?" I asked, grimacing as I heard my question aloud and got the full brunt of its crassness. "Not to insinuate you would die in battle … it's just so many did."

Asher shrugged, waving a hand to show me my question hadn't offended him. His gesture also reminded me he wouldn't have any idea why Sully might've wanted him to die, since spirits don't remember the time surrounding their death. For this reason, many ghosts sought the help of a human medium—which is what I guess I was—to help them uncover the truth about how they died and settle their unfinished business.

"If anyone in Pebble Cove hated me enough to kill me, it was Sully Mills." He said it as if it were irrefutable, a fact.

"If that's true, why are you still here?" I asked, cocking an eyebrow at him.

Asher paused, taken aback by the dryness in my tone.

"You solved it," I said. "And yet you're still here in front of me. Why haven't you moved on?" That was blunt, but I'd found when it came to Sully, Asher had the tendency to be stubborn and bullheaded too—as he had accused his nemesis.

Asher cleared his throat. Obviously the reaction was more of a habit carried over from his life as he no longer had a physical throat or anything to clear from it, but it spoke volumes. I'd flustered him.

"I haven't figured out specifically why Sully killed me or any of the details yet. Maybe I need to find out all of that." Asher tried to hold my gaze, but I could tell by the way his eyes kept darting around the room that he got my point.

My ghostly friend was a humble and kind person. I'd only seen this angry, vindictive side of him come out when we talked of Sully or Abigail. This wasn't like him, and I tried to give him the benefit of the doubt.

"If it was Sully," I said in a move to be a little more conciliatory with my friend, "how are we going to find proof? It was a hundred years ago."

Asher rubbed a hand over his chin in contemplation.

"Good question. Local newspapers and town records wouldn't likely have anything helpful. We'll most likely be looking for personal items of Sully's or stories passed down from people who knew him," Asher said, sending me a blank look to show he had no idea where to find any of that.

I yawned. "Well, we can start on figuring out that mystery tomorrow. Some of us need to get some sleep around here." I got up, taking the wool blanket with me.

Asher nodded. "Goodnight, Rosemary."

"See you in the morning. Don't spend all night thinking about the Mills family," I said as I padded over to where he sat in his favorite armchair. I kissed my fingers, then placed them onto his forehead—well, where his forehead appeared to me. My fingers felt cool where we met, but there was no resistance.

He smiled up at me, but as I left him in the library, I feared Asher's thoughts would be akin to the darkening clouds offshore, brewing something dangerous and destructive.

The next day, I woke to find Asher gone. After a few minutes of searching, I spotted him out on the beach, staring out at the waves. I didn't have time to talk to him because I opened the tea shop to a line of customers. Texts from Jolene proved she had a similar influx of patrons, demonstrating she'd been correct about the locals coming to us for the gossip.

Now that the gossip had to do with a young woman's murder, however, the idea of trading rumors didn't sound as appealing. So I stuck to telling people about the yurts and the changes Van had made to the property. I could tell my avoidance of the murder was losing me some points with the locals, with whom information worked almost like currency. But they were good people, and they understood chatting about Clover's death as if it were simply another local happening would be crass.

Still, whispered questions about the girl's murder served as the background to the soundtrack of my day. It was a low hum acting as a bass note, something you don't notice until it's gone.

And at about lunchtime, it disappeared. Suddenly. The room went quiet. Well, not completely quiet, but that low whisper was gone, replaced by a cheery, fake-sounding conversational tone.

I glanced up from behind the tea bar to see the reason all talk of the murder at The Pines had stopped. Van Mills walked toward me. And even though he was still handsome as ever, he was missing the polished aspect of his appearance. He wore the same clothes as he'd worn last night at the festival, and he looked like he hadn't slept a minute in between.

"Rosemary, hello." His voice strained. He coughed before continuing. "I'm so sorry about last night."

He didn't qualify that by adding what he was sorry about. The murder? His disappearance? But the man seemed too tired and too run down, so I didn't push.

"I'm so sorry about what happened to one of your guests. Is there anything I can do to help?" I busied myself with setting a customer's order to steep, glad for the physical distraction.

"You and Jolene can cater the healing ceremony we're having tomorrow."

I blinked up at him.

"The guests said you and Jolene were such a comfort yesterday, serving the tea and desserts," he added after I said nothing. "Tomorrow afternoon at three. We're having a memorial service for Clover. Bring whatever tea you want, and Jolene can make anything she likes."

I chewed on my lip, my thoughts sticking on Asher's accusations about Van being the killer. Discomfort climbed up my skin, leaving goosebumps in its wake. Realizing the tea shop had gone almost silent in the background, I peeked around Van. The dozen or so customers shifted their focus elsewhere, and the pretend conversations started back up as cover.

This kind of scrutiny used to give me heart palpitations. The reaction was a holdout from my fight with leukemia as a child and the way people used to stare and whisper about me. But after being in Pebble Cove for the better part of a year, I was moving beyond those anxieties.

"Okay," I said with a quick nod. "I'll talk to Jolene and call you for the details."

Color filled Van's features again. Placing his hand over mine on the tea bar, he squeezed tight. "I knew you were my favorite tea shop owner for a reason. I'll look forward to your call. I promise no one will die this time."

And with that, he left. His last statement made my skin go cold. How could he guarantee that? Was it because he'd been the one to kill yesterday?

Once the door closed, the whispered bass line returned to the conversations, and I relaxed into the normalcy. That was, until I closed and Asher cornered me.

"You're going back?" he asked, eyebrows knit so far forward it was as if they pointed accusingly at me.

I gathered the dishes from the tea shop so it didn't seem

like I was avoiding making eye contact. "I thought you were on the beach all day. How'd you hear that?"

Asher folded his arms over his chest. "I saw Van coming inside, so I did too."

"That's a very casual way of saying you spied on me," I said, raising an eyebrow.

Asher huffed out an exhale. "I don't spy on you, Rosie. I'm worried. And it looks like I need to be since you accepted his invitation."

"Asher, come on. I'll be fine." I loaded the first round into the dishwasher.

"That's what you said last time, and it wasn't. You've accepted an invitation from a murderer to return to the scene of a crime. Do you think this will end well?"

I sighed. I wasn't about to let him know how Van's statement about no one dying this time had rubbed me the wrong way. "If you take out the part about Van being the murderer—because you have no way to prove it's true—then I'm accepting an invitation to help a community heal after a tragedy. And I'm going to do it." Loading the last plate into the rack, I closed the dishwasher and started it running.

He stayed silent after that but didn't appear happy.

"I'll be careful," I said, softening my tone. "I promise."

"I do not trust that family." Asher's expression loosened from its taut state.

"I know. But I thought about our conundrum, about getting information about your death. Me spending time around Van, and his house, will be one of the best ways for us to look into whether or not Sully was the one who killed you."

Asher clenched his jaw. "I don't like it at all, but I also know how difficult it is to talk you out of something once you've set your mind to it." His eyes met mine. "I appreciate your willingness to help. I wish it didn't come at the price of your safety."

But even as I assured Asher it wouldn't, a chill wound through my chest, tightening around my lungs, making me doubt if I was right.

6

The rest of the day was bleak and rainy. An October storm pelted Pebble Cove with an unyielding blanket of slashing rain. Whether it was the storm we'd noticed last night or a different one, I couldn't be sure.

All I knew was that I had to bring in all the outdoor cushions from the deck and turn on the furnace for the first time since I'd moved in.

Asher and I hunkered inside, starting a new book together. We were reading this month's pick for our Tea by the Sea book club, *The Mysterious Benedict Society* by Trenton Lee Stewart. This month Mom had picked a children's novel, assuring us it was a wonderful adventure fit for all ages.

The author's words filled the room as wind and rain ravaged the coastline outside the windows. It almost felt as if the storm was looking in, tapping at the glass with droplet fingertips, asking to come inside so it might listen along.

The storm raged through the night, but by lunchtime the next day, the clouds had receded, and the sun's rays were doing their best to clean up the wet mess.

Water vapor rose from the pea gravel in the tea shop parking lot as Jolene and I loaded our catering supplies into her car for the second time. We did it all again, driving up to The Pines, parking near the tables, carrying our boxes of supplies.

I couldn't speak for Jolene, but it felt like a surreal dream to set up just as we had the other night. Jolene brought scones and cookies instead of the cakes and moon pies, but my chamomile tea blend was the same. And even though the tea had a light, floral taste, memories of the last time I'd served it made the liquid bitter on my tongue as I sipped a sample.

To my surprise, Cinder was back among the group. He attended the healing ceremony but sat in the back and avoided making eye contact. I wondered why the chief hadn't arrested him yet. Based on the clues I'd learned, he seemed to be the prime suspect.

I reminded myself that in the other cases I'd worked on, the prime suspect wasn't always the one who ended up guilty. Was it possible Cinder had an alibi? Maybe it was Van. What if my guess had been correct, and they actually had spent their time away from the group working out whatever issues they seemed to have.

But if it wasn't Cinder, who was the killer?

My attention swept over the group. Meadow seemed to have composed herself from the other night. She looked somber and sad with her brown hair braided back off her pale face.

Jolene and I stayed away, observing as they threw flowers onto the ground, sang songs, and a few got up to speak about Clover.

"Clover was the coolest girl I've ever known," said the girl who'd been wearing the thick headband the other night.

"She was an unapologetic artist and a beautiful wordsmith. I wish I'd been able to get to know her better."

Others stood to comment on Clover's beauty, insight, and artistic soul, repeating the first girl's sentiment. She was a writer, it sounded, some quoting her poetry, others talking about her knack for finding just the right motivational quote for any situation. All of them held her in such high regard for only having known her a month.

As I watched the ceremony, I realized that everyone here was around my age. Jolene, in her forties, was probably the oldest person present. I knew Van was in his mid-twenties like me, and everyone else seemed to fit that description. Cinder looked like he might be in his thirties, but that might've been a trick from the way his face wrinkled with a constant scowl.

His attitude during the ceremony only piled more suspicion onto him. Who sat in the back at a loved one's memorial and refused to speak?

The ceremony had wrapped up, most of the food and tea was gone, and the guests milled about our tables, when Chief Clemenson's SUV pulled up the long driveway. It wasn't until the chief climbed out and Van walked over to meet him I realized I hadn't seen Cinder since we'd started serving food. My focus had turned to pouring tea and refilling boiling water. In the midst, I'd lost track of him.

"I'm going to go talk to the chief real quick," I told Jolene, setting an empty tea kettle in the box. I needed to tell him about my kettle and the fact that it hadn't been used as the murder weapon.

As I approached the policeman and property owner, the chief leaned in close to ask Van a question as he searched the crowd. Clemenson's attention caught on me. He shot me an exasperated "Stay out of this, Woodmere" glare. The way he glanced past me and continued to search for someone else confirmed this might not be the best of times. Van looked, too, shielding his eyes from the brightness that a sky full of white clouds can give off, not having the protection of a hat brim like the chief. The longer they scanned without finding what—or who—they were looking for, the more Van's features creased in concern.

The chief said something into his radio and asked Van another question. Van pointed to the line of yurts along the edge of the property and Clemenson took off. I returned to the tables, wondering when I'd get a chance to let the chief know about my kettle.

Jolene and I busied ourselves with cleaning and packing up as the rest of the community members dispersed. I wasn't sure if they'd gone back to their yurts hoping to catch a glimpse of what the chief was doing or if they wanted to give him privacy. But judging from the way they huddled and whispered on their way back to their sites, I guessed it was the former.

And they had quite a lot to whisper about thirty minutes later when the chief walked Cinder over to his SUV. Well, it wasn't so much of a walk as it was a shove. Cinder shouted things like, "I didn't do it!" and "You've got the wrong guy!" as the chief pushed him toward his vehicle. The metal glint of handcuffs from behind Cinder's back sparked my interest even more.

"You could've avoided all of this if you had answered my questions," Chief Clemenson said loudly enough for us to hear before they got inside his SUV and drove away.

We'd packed the last bit of our supplies into the car when Van came over, holding a check out like a white flag.

"Sorry about all of that." He flapped the check in the direction of the driveway. "I hoped we would at least get through her memorial without more drama, but I get that the law waits for no one." His grim expression turned friendly as he handed over the check. "Everyone loved the refreshments. Thank you."

Jolene and I thanked him, especially when we both caught sight of the amount written on the check Jolene clutched in her hand.

Van rubbed a hand over the back of his neck. "Uh, Rosemary, I don't know if you have plans this evening, but there's something I'd love to talk with you about if you don't mind staying. I'll drive you home later."

Asher's worried warnings from last night echoed through my mind.

Van must've recognized my hesitation because he added, "Totally up to you, of course. If not, I can come talk down at the tea shop some other time."

Between the way his shoulders drooped and dark circles had spread under his usually bright eyes, I wondered if he just wanted some company.

Jolene, having encouraged me to pursue something with Van from the start, looked like she wanted to shove me toward him. "I can drop your stuff off at Tea by the Sea," she said with a gleam in her eye.

Swallowing a groan, I realized that my supplies coming back without me would be a red flag for Asher. But my house wasn't far out of her way home, and it made little sense for me to suggest she take all of my stuff back to her house either, so I was stuck.

"Thank you," I said to Jolene. Then I turned and said, "Sure, I can stay," to Van.

"Perfect," Van said, a grin spreading across his face as he gestured for me to follow him.

Jolene and I parted ways, but not before she leveled me

with a look that said, in no uncertain terms, that I would need to report every detail to her tonight when I got home. I waved goodbye and followed Van.

The crunching of Jolene's tires on the driveway faded as her car rounded the first bend, leaving only the peaceful songs of birds in the surrounding trees, the distant roar of the ocean, and the rustling of leaves as the wind picked up again. The sky turned murky. I zipped up my jacket, having learned my lesson from the chill I'd gotten the other night.

"Thanks for staying," Van said as we walked toward the house. "My sister had to go back to the city yesterday, and I'm craving company after everything that's happened over the past few days."

"I bet. Did you know any of these people before they came to stay here?"

Van stopped and turned his attention to the yurts dotting the extensive property. "A couple of them, but mostly they found me through word of mouth."

A couple of them. My brain latched on to that phrase.

"Was Cinder one of them?" I asked, following his gaze out into the field.

He waited until he'd pulled in a lengthy breath before saying, "Yeah, we've known each other for about a year. I feel awful because I invited him to come. I thought he would be a positive addition to the community. The guy's a total health food nut and runs a vegan blog that gets thousands of hits a day, not to mention the sponsors he's gotten through Instagram and Youtube reviewing products and sharing recipes and workout tips."

That made sense. Cinder's fitness was hard to look past. It had been there first thing I'd noticed about him—besides his temper, that is. Of course people would want to follow his exercise and meal plans.

Van's lips pinched together. "I knew about his anger issues. I didn't think they would be a problem here though, you know?" He turned to me. "It's so peaceful, and there's nothing to worry about. At least, that's what I wanted to achieve … it just didn't work." Van's normal confidence seemed to leak out of him like air out of a punctured balloon.

People milled about in the communal garden area, chatting and working in the earth. Another group pulled out instruments and began playing a song I didn't recognize. If I didn't know there had been a murder here a couple of nights before, it would've seemed like a peaceful paradise.

"So you think Cinder did it?" I asked, glancing up at the gray clouds moving overhead.

Van shrugged. "It's the only thing that makes sense. I think he lied about his alibi, so that's why they're bringing him in. At least, that's the impression I got from all the questions the chief asked me about when and where I'd seen him that night."

So Cinder hadn't been with Van then or else he would've had an alibi. Interesting.

I itched to be a fly on the wall in that interrogation room with the chief and Cinder. With a smile, I realized I didn't need to be a fly. One of the local spirits, Lois, could listen in for me. Instantly regretting my decision to stay here, I wished I was headed downtown right now to ask her to poke around for me.

But because I was here, I made the best use of my time. "It's so weird that he would've hurt Clover since it seemed like he was mad at you instead." I tried to keep my tone light and conversational despite the heavy thing I insinuated. "What was he so mad at you about, anyway?"

Van's face paled. "He found out I was going to ask him

to leave." As if he knew that wasn't going to be enough, Van added, "He wasn't really upholding the 'peaceful' part of a peaceful living community."

From the interaction I'd had with Cinder, I couldn't blame Van. And if things had gotten bad enough that Van was willing to kick him out, the fight someone overheard Cinder and Clover having after dinner that night must not have been the first of its kind.

Before I could ask any follow up questions, a buzzing sound came from Van's back pocket. "Sorry," he said, patting the pocket before grabbing out his phone. "I've got to take this." He glanced up at me.

I waved a hand toward his phone, motioning that he shouldn't worry about me.

Van turned his attention to his phone, answering the call as he jogged up the steps to the white farmhouse. "Hey, thanks for calling me back," was all I heard before the front door closed behind him.

The chill in the air worsened as the clouds above moved further on the gray scale toward black. My jacket still kept me plenty warm, however, so I was happy to wait outside.

That was until I spotted someone at the tree line.

A very concerned-looking man, wearing tweed pants, suspenders, and frown lines I could see from here, paced off in the distance.

Asher.

Jolene must've dropped off my supplies. Worried I wasn't with them, he must've come here to check on me. Glancing back toward the house, I didn't see any sign of Van. I probably had a few minutes until he came back. I had time to go talk to Asher, to calm his fears.

I walked toward the tree line.

And I would've gone all the way to him if I hadn't heard

the sounds of someone sniffling as I passed by the first yurt. I paused and listened, trying not to be rude. The fabric door of the yurt was drawn open, and a quiet sob flowed, unimpeded, to my ears.

I held up a finger to show Asher I would be there in a minute and headed for the tent. "Hello?" I called into the opening. "Are you okay in here?"

Stepping forward when I didn't hear an answer, I caught sight of Meadow sitting on the bed in the middle of her yurt. Her face was splotched and red.

She met my gaze and broke into a new round of sobs.

7

"Hey, hey. It's okay." I walked into Meadow's yurt, grabbing a tissue from a box on a dresser.

The tissue was brown, like it was made from recycled material, but it felt soft enough to do the job. I handed it to her as I approached.

"Thanks," she wailed through another sob before burying her face into the tissue and blowing her nose.

A beautiful floral quilt covered the bed she sat on. It looked handmade, like the one I still hadn't had the heart to move off my late grandmother's untouched bed.

In fact, Clover's yurt being the only other I'd seen inside, Meadow's space seemed to be as different as was possible. They both appeared to have the same basic pieces in the tent like the large rug, bed, dresser, desk, a hot plate, water cooler, and a couple of camping lamps hanging here and there. Van must've advertised them as furnished yurts, so guests didn't have to bring much.

Meadow's belongings differed completely from Clover's. Whereas Clover's yurt had looked like something out of an influencer's Instagram post, everything curated to create a certain impression, Meadow's space seemed to be a cozy compilation of everything she loved most in the world. Her frames held pictures of actual people instead of obscure art, like Clover's had. There was even an entire board filled with Polaroid pictures and a plastic container in the corner which looked like it contained a bunch more, judging by the white along the edges.

Odd. That was a lot of printed pictures, especially for a digital-loving millennial like Meadow. But I'd seen a resurgence of using "vintage" cameras like Polaroids lately, so it wasn't too strange.

"What's going on?" I asked, sitting next to her on the bed.

Meadow sniffed, the wet sound confirming her need to blow her nose again. Her face crumpled into discomfort, like she either couldn't say what was wrong or knew explaining would make her cry even harder.

"Is it Clover?" I asked.

Even though Meadow hadn't seemed overly distraught during the healing ceremony today, she'd been the one to find Clover's body. As someone who'd seen a dead body before, I knew it wasn't something you easily forgot, or got over. She'd also said they planned to go to the festival together, so they had been at least sort of close.

But Meadow shook her head. "No. I mean, it's awful what happened to her."

Admitting she wasn't crying for Clover seemed to make her sob even harder, though, and I waited for her to catch her breath again.

A few moments later, Meadow pulled in a shuddery breath and swiped the tissue across her nose. "You're the caterer, right? Why are you still here?" she asked, almost like an accusation.

"Van wanted to discuss some business with me, but he got called away for a second, and I heard you crying." I shrugged.

Her face crumpled again at the reminder she'd been crying, but she held it together this time, taking a deep breath. "I'm worried about Cinder," she said through a sigh.

"Cinder?" My eyebrows and tone rose simultaneously.

Meadow erupted into a fresh bout of sobs. "I'm the reason the police just took him," she wailed.

"What? Why?"

Meadow glanced at the door to her yurt, making sure no one was outside. "I'm his alibi. I was with him." The way she whispered *with him* made me sure the two of them hadn't been working on craft projects together.

"Shouldn't that mean he wouldn't be in trouble, though?" I asked.

She sniffled back tears. "Well, he was here most of the time, I think. I fell asleep, and when I woke up, he was gone."

Oh, so that's why the chief had taken him down to the station. If he'd used Meadow as his alibi and they questioned her, finding out he wasn't with her during the whole time in question, that didn't look good for Cinder.

"I love him. I know he didn't do anything like that." Meadow glanced down at her hands in her lap.

I eyed her, not sharing her confidence in the man.

"He was dating Clover, though," I said, realizing the naïveté of my question when Meadow's expression softened.

We were probably the same age—in fact, I might have had a year or two on the girl—but while my childhood had been all treatments and condolences and sheltering for my own good, I was sure that look meant Meadow had more experience.

She shook her head. "Neither of them believed in 'relationships,'" Meadow said, using finger quotes around that last word as if she were talking about something make-believe, like unicorns. "They had an open thing going. Had since the first day we all got here."

Scrunching my toes in my boots while I thought this through, I wondered if that kind of thing ever worked out. Clover's death seemed to be proof that it didn't.

"What if Cinder wasn't okay with it? Was she seeing other guys?" I asked.

Meadow nodded.

"What if he found out and snapped?" I suggested, remembering his tornado-inside-a-bottle countenance the other night.

"No, there's no way." She cut the air with her hand, the gesture losing much of its desired finality because she still clutched the used tissue in that hand.

"Okay," I said, seeing this conversation wasn't going anywhere else. "Well, hang in there. I'd better go check on Van." I jabbed my thumb toward the door.

Meadow waved goodbye, and I got out of there before I became even more confused. A quick glance at the house told me Van hadn't come back outside, so I skirted around Meadow's yurt and toward the tree line.

Asher paced at the edge of the grass, wearing a disgruntled expression as plainly as his suspenders. About to scold him for coming to check in on me, for not trusting me, the relief in his face when he spotted me made me hold my tongue. A smile lit up his blue eyes, and his ghostly shoulders relaxed.

"What were you doing in there?" he asked, gesturing to Meadow's yurt.

"Learning that they took Cinder away in handcuffs

because he lied about his alibi. He must've expected Meadow to cover for him, but she very well gave them the thing they needed to put him away." I tucked my chin into my jacket collar, noticing the weather had gotten even worse since I'd made my detour.

"Have you told the chief about the kettle yet?" he asked.

"I tried, but he was busy." I gave Asher a conspiratorial eyebrow waggle. "I'm thinking I'll drive there when I'm done here and let him know. And if I run into Lois downtown and she happens to have heard anything in the interrogation room, that's just luck, isn't it? And if I learn nothing, it's no big deal since this whole thing doesn't really have anything to do with me."

Asher chuckled. "Okay, well, I'll see you back at home, then. Just wanted to make sure you were safe."

I studied him, realizing he wasn't as transparent as I would expect him to be this far from home. Then it clicked … where we stood. Any pleasant feelings brought up by seeing Asher vanished. My heart sank, and my stomach flipped as my eyes landed on the freshly packed soil that delineated a large rectangle in the earth. It was the size and shape of a grave.

"Asher, is this where …" I couldn't finish the sentence, instead sucking in a breath.

Somber, he surveyed the area. "Yeah. This is it."

Sadness and shock fought to be the reaction that won out as I stared at the place where Asher's body had been buried until a few months ago.

Seemingly unaffected, he waved me over. "Let me show you that cool tree I was telling you about."

I fought to match his laid-back attitude about it all. "The one you and your friends hid in to make your coyote sounds?" I asked with a snort.

He adopted an impish grin. They had pulled quite a few trees to expand the property, but in this part of the yard it appeared the large tree Asher had been buried next to had been the only one taken down to help keep some privacy between the driveway and the yurts.

He led me over to a trunk probably twenty feet tall, which lightning had obviously struck. The top was charred and jagged in a way that made it seem like the rest of the tree had exploded into charred dust on impact. Other than that, the trunk seemed solid as any other.

Asher walked me around the tree counterclockwise, the way that made sense if we came from the property. Nothing seemed amiss about the trunk at all. Asher held up a finger, leading us back around the trunk. This time, we walked clockwise. From this direction, he walked until he touched the trunk—or would've touched it if he had a body.

I still didn't see what he was doing, but before I knew what happened, he disappeared. The guy disappeared all the time, though, so unless he'd told me what to expect about the tree, I wouldn't have gone closer to investigate.

Sure enough, once I came at it with just the right angle, an opening showed itself in front of me. It must've been the bark creating the illusion.

"How'd you find this?" I asked in a hoarse whisper once the entrance spilled me into the hollowed interior of the trunk. It was damp and smelled like rotting earth, but it held a timeless peacefulness. I was also quite certain this was where every spider in the surrounding woods must live and told myself not to study the barky walls around me too hard.

"We used to come up through the woods, that way," he said, pointing straight out where we'd entered. "When you're lower than the tree, like you are walking up the path, you can see there's a break in the bark. Sully used to come out here and search but never found us."

I couldn't help but find his boyish enthusiasm endearing. "Well, speaking of Sullivan Mills searching for people, I should get back to Van. He's probably wondering where I went."

To Asher's credit, he only made a half-sour face at my mention of Van. We left the decomposing trunk and headed back for the large farmhouse. Van stood on the porch scanning the grounds. He still had the phone glued to his ear, but when he caught sight of me, he motioned with his free hand, beckoning me to join him.

"Rosie," Asher said, stopping me before I left.

I tensed, waiting for him to tell me not to go, urging me to come back home.

"Be careful," he said.

I nodded and went to join Van.

8

Van waved as I climbed the stairs and joined him on the large wraparound porch. He pointed to his phone and twirled one finger in the air, miming that he was wrapping it up.

I stood next to him for a moment, leaning on the railing. But an angry, charcoal cloud covered the sky, and my jacket was no longer up to the task of keeping the bite in the air from digging its freezing fangs into me.

It was also odd listening in on someone else's conversation. Even Van seemed self-conscious, looking at me out of the corner of his eye and obviously choosing his words carefully.

Shivering, I pointed inside. Van nodded.

The closest door leading in from the porch spit me into the kitchen. Memories of my time spent here with Althea Pine, the woman who I'd thought was a friend of my grandmother's but was actually her killer, crowded around me like monsters in a nightmare.

Walking forward, I wanted nothing more than to leave

the kitchen. There had to be a library in a grand old house like this. Maybe I would feel more at home there.

But as I passed by the industrial, stainless steel countertop, something caught my eye. A notepad and pen sat near the edge as if Van had been scribbling reminders for himself. The notepad was flipped upside down.

I glanced behind me, out the porch window. Van's back was still to me, his focus still on his phone call. So I crept closer to the counter, flipped over the pad, and eyed the scratchy penmanship. Three questions were written on the pad:

Does my plan cover if the item is lost? How much of the money will I get back? Should I say it was stolen?

The last question had a thin, almost imperceptible line drawn through it as if Van had decided against asking it. His written queries made one question spring up in my mind.

What had Van lost? The plan he referenced sounded like an insurance policy. If that were true, it must be something expensive.

Footsteps out on the porch snapped my focus away from the notepad. Not wanting to get caught snooping through his stuff, I flipped the pad back over, took a large step closer to the oven, and pretended to be interested in the fancy appliance.

The exterior door opened as I was fiddling with the knobs on the range. I looked over at Van who schooled his expression into a smile when he noticed me.

"Great oven, isn't it?" He let the door close behind him and strode over to me.

I racked my brain for what I could possibly find interesting about this stove.

"I think you could fit a whole person in here." I laughed

awkwardly. "If you were the witch in *Hansel and Gretel*, that is." My cheeks heated up.

Why did I say that? I scolded myself. *That was the creepiest possible compliment.*

Instead of slapping my hand onto my forehead, I stood and took a step back from the oven, hoping if we weren't close to it we might move the conversation to something else.

Van didn't seem to find my comment creepy at all. "Makes it even more of a shame that I can't cook to save my life, huh?"

I took another step back. "Your phone call go okay?" I asked, hoping to change the subject.

Van's amiable smile took on a forced nature as he said, "Yeah, sorry about that. Just some business stuff I had to take care of."

"No problem," I said quickly. "I had a nice time exploring around the property. It's so pretty up here."

Sighing, Van turned to look out the window. "It really is, isn't it?"

"It's great the place is back in your family." I leaned back on the counter, my back to the notepad with the confusing questions. "I inherited my house too, you know."

He raised his eyebrows. "That's nice. I love it here. I'm sure that's why my dad left it to me. Either that or he was trying to punish me." Van let out a wry laugh.

"Punish you? How would giving you a beautiful house and property be a punishment?" I asked.

Van stepped closer, leaning onto the counter next to me. "He used to say this place was full of ghosts."

Eyebrows jumping at this statement, I tried to temper my reaction. "Like, bad memories?" I asked for clarification, not having seen any actual ghosts here.

"I guess. He and his father didn't get along at all. He never knew his grandfather, but I think he kind of idolized the man, built him up to be everything his father wasn't." Van rolled his eyes. "The infallible Sully."

I swallowed, wanting him to keep talking so badly the anticipation practically hummed in my veins. "Your great-grandfather?" I asked, pretending like I was trying to track with the information he'd given me, not that I'd already heard a lot about Sully from Asher.

"Yes, in the long line of Sullivan Mills, my father thought the first was the greatest," he sneered.

Squinting one eye, I said, "You're *all* called Sullivan Mills?"

"Sully was my great-grandfather; my grandfather went by SJ, Sullivan Junior. My father went by Ivan Mills instead of going with his *third* title."

I thought for a second then said, "Sull*ivan*. Got it."

"And I'm technically the fifth person named Sullivan in our family. I like Van better. I don't have a title since my dad decided instead of just naming his firstborn Sullivan, he wanted us all to have the name." A large inhale lifted his chest.

Cocking my head to one side. "All?" I asked, only having met his sister.

Van rubbed at his temples. "My poor sister got dragged into this. She's Sullivan the fourth. I'm plain old Sullivan Mills since she was born first."

I took that in. "Liv is short for Sullivan?"

He laughed in that way you do when it's the only way you know how to deal with something that makes little sense. "She's a real trooper, my big sister."

I remembered how focused on looking out for her brother she was. It was good to see that. Even though he hadn't had the greatest relationship with his father, he still had a wonderful connection to his sister.

"Seems like you guys look out for each other."

Van scoffed, "I'd be lucky if I could ever help her out. Liv ends up saving my butt all the time. Whether she was defending my choices to our father or now that she'll probably have to bail me out of this mess, she's got my back."

Wetting my lips, I carefully asked, "Bail you out of *this* mess?"

He turned his attention out to the yurts. "This place was going to take years to be profitable in the first place, something my father would've forbidden putting money into. But with his death, Liv became CEO of our family company. Liv got our father's business sense, but she's still a good sister. She loaned me the money. And now that someone's been murdered here, I'll have a heck of a time getting anyone else to come here." Van's posture slumped. "The worst part is knowing my father was right about how I would never make anything stick."

I cringed. I'd lost my father in a car accident when I was a kid and I still missed him every day. My mom and I definitely didn't have a perfect relationship. But I felt so grateful that I'd never felt like I'd disappointed her with what I was doing with my life or how I was choosing to live it. I wished I could be at home, calling my mom and chatting with her about the day.

"I'm so sorry," I said, meeting Van's troubled gaze. "That's an awful way to feel."

He ran a hand through his hair. "The worst part is that I've always wanted to do something that proves our family cares about more than money, but those endeavors usually end up meaning my family has to bail me out." He sighed. "I wanted this place to be different."

I wished Asher could hear this. Not only could he relate to Van's difficult relationship with his father—having never quite lived up to who his father wished he would be either—but also because this was proof that Van couldn't be Clover's killer. A death in his community would mean the death of his dream. If this was the worst thing he could imagine, he definitely wouldn't have been the one to throw it all away.

"The people here seem happy," I offered. "They don't seem like they're about to run away."

He swiped a hand through his hair, but the pain I caught in his eyes as he looked away from me was hard to witness. In my discomfort, I studied the rest of the kitchen, noting how it had changed from the last time I'd been here, back when the place was a restorative center. The large metal shelving unit had stayed, but it was full of fancy-looking, specialized culinary gadgets instead of the more rustic tools Althea and her cook had used.

He had three iterations of some sort of a handheld coffee press, a very shiny—like it was unused, shiny—espresso machine, and … my breath caught in my throat … a half dozen of the cast-iron kettles. The same ones he'd purchased for me and my catering supplies.

Following my line of sight, he said, "Oh, I ended up purchasing some of my own too, liked them so much when I was ordering yours." He reached out and picked one up, turning it in his hands. "I'm not some crazy tea kettle collector or anything. I like to have enough of these for people to take back to their yurts if they want."

"So this equipment is open to anyone?" I asked around the frog in my throat.

Van returned the kettle with jerky movements. "Yeah. They can come by and check them out, but most people use them in the kitchen. The yurts leave a little to be desired in the way of culinary endeavors."

I remembered seeing the hot plate in Meadow's yurt earlier.

"There are only five here," I said, taking a step toward the shelf as I noticed an empty spot next to the line of kettles. "Are there more checked out, or is this all of them?"

Van rubbed at his chin. "I definitely ordered six." The moment he realized why one was missing registered on his face. "Oh." Van cleared his throat, looking at me.

I pressed my lips together.

But the worry that had taken hold of Van's features loosened. "There's a log. I forgot to mention that to the chief. Let's see if the person who checked one out used the log like I told them to." He reached for a clipboard hanging from the shelving unit, a pen attached by a long string.

Excitement built inside me as he angled the clipboard toward us. This could be a clue as to who might've killed Clover. But even though the sheet was broken into columns including the borrower's name, the date borrowed, and the date returned, no one had written on any of the lines.

Van's shoulders slumped in defeat as if he was more disappointed in the fact they weren't following the rules instead of how the missing kettle had definitely been used to kill a woman a couple of days prior.

"I'll have to talk with them about writing their names in the future," he said, but his statement petered out at the end. If he was right about the effects of Clover's death on his community dream, there might very well not be a future.

All this talk about kettles was just one more sign that I needed to let Chief Clemenson know that it wasn't one of mine that had been used. Which meant I needed to get home so I could drive myself to the station. Maybe I would get there in time and Cinder would still be in one of the interrogation rooms.

I smiled sympathetically at Van as I checked my watch. "Sorry, I should get back home. What did you want to talk with me about? Can we chat in the car?"

Van's eyes widened. "Oh, right. Sorry, I almost forgot." He gestured out to the parking lot. "Yes, let's talk in the car. Mostly I wanted to ask if you would be interested in selling me some of your teas in bulk to use here in the community."

My feet faltered as we walked through the front door. I passed it off as an accident, acting as if I'd tripped on the threshold.

His proposition should've been welcome. Another avenue to sell my teas should make me happy. But his proposal made me feel light headed. The last person to ask for such a business relationship with me had been a murderer.

My disorientation only increased as we stepped out from under the cover of the porch, and wind pelted us with stinging cold droplets of rain. Van and I ran for the car he pointed out as his.

"Selling my tea here sounds great," I said as we climbed into his car.

And as much time as I'd spent convincing myself that Van was innocent in this whole crime, I couldn't help that a few things about him were too similar to Althea and her friendly façade.

I swallowed my fear as we drove toward my house. Maybe Asher's non-gut gut feeling was right after all.

9

Relief rushed over me as I exited Van's car and waved goodbye. Simply looking at my house made me feel warm already.

I ran for cover under the front awning, glancing for a moment at the gloomy clouds gathering overhead. The rain intensified as if I'd challenged the clouds with my acknowledgment and they were proving they were serious.

Jolene had set my box of catering supplies safely under the front awning. Heaving the box onto my hip, I pushed my way inside after unlocking the door. The house smelled like a mixture of dried leaves and sugar. I wanted to stop and breathe it all in. Honestly, I wanted to curl up on the couch with a book and a cup of tea.

But the police station called to me.

Asher appeared in the tearoom as I jogged in, my wet shoes squeaking on the wood floors. I set the box on the floor and waved as I turned to leave.

"Everything okay?" he asked, looking me up and down to make sure I was in one piece.

I stopped and turned back to him. "Yeah, I just want to hop over to the police station. Wanna come with?"

Usually Asher was all for trips into town, but today his expression clouded over, much like the sky above. "Rosie, I don't think you should go out in this weather. It's terrible out there." He checked out the window, and the rain intensified even more.

Being from Portland, I wasn't scared of a little rain. I wrinkled my nose. "It's fine, Ash. I have to tell the chief about my kettle, and the fact that one of the communal kettles Van kept in the kitchen was missing."

Asher's eyebrows lifted with interest.

I held up a finger. "Not because Van used it, but one of the community members did."

Asher cocked his head to one side, seeming dubious about that fact. The reminder of his distrust in the man gave fuel to the thoughts of doubt that had cropped up during my conversation with Van.

"Okay, I'll admit some things about Van do not seem to add up. But I'm not willing to call him a murderer. We can talk more about it when I get back, but I want to make it to the station while Cinder is still there so the chief can ask him about the kettle and the different timeline." I grabbed my car keys from a hook in the hallway, then I paused and glanced back. "You coming with?" I asked.

"Can't you just call him?" Asher asked, but sighed as he realized the answer. How would I be able to snoop around if I called? His blue eyes pierced mine with worry and frustration. But he nodded. "I'll meet you down there." Then he vanished.

Running out to my car after locking the tea shop door, I wished I'd grabbed an umbrella. My jacket was soaked in the couple-yard dash from the tea shop to my car. I started the wipers on high and backed up, heading for town.

But I didn't even make it halfway down the easement road between my house and Carl's before something confusing stopped me.

Carl, it seemed, was dressed up just like the Gorton's fisherman. His head-to-toe yellow rain suit was alarming enough, but when he ran in front of my car, arms waving, I stopped. Rain streamed off his matching yellow hat as he came around to my driver's side window and bent to talk to me.

"Rosie, wherever you're going has to wait. There's a storm coming. We've got to batten down!" The sound of the rain pelting my metal roof, and the crashing of waves churned up by the wind made it so he had to yell even though we were only feet apart.

Squinting against the raindrops finding their way into my car through my open window, I pointed. "I have to go to the police station to talk to the chief," I yelled back. "It's important."

Carl shook his head, flinging more water into my car. "Not more important than your life. Misty Drive has the tendency to flood, and either you'll get washed off the road or stuck in town. If I were you, I'd stay put. Have you squall-proofed your house?"

I blinked, both against the rain and the confusing question. "What's that?"

Carl waved his arm back toward my house like someone directing an airplane. "Back up. I'll help you."

Staying put for a moment, I stared at Misty Drive ahead, at the way to town, to the station, to answers. But adding to my recent anecdotal proof that the weather had a sentient personality of its own, it chose that moment to start the hail.

I rolled up my window and backed up as Carl ran along-side my car. I huddled under the awning with him for a moment once I'd parked my car. Thunder cracked through the sky, adding urgency to our movements.

We started on the deck, putting away the furniture—one chair had already blown into the garden. And it only took me five minutes out in the storm to decide I needed to ask Carl where he'd bought his rain gear.

Carl left to "batten down" his own house when Asher appeared. The cozy dry clothes I'd changed into and kettle set to boil for tea painted such a calm picture. So when Asher's spirit flashed into the room, his wide eyes and worried attitude felt more fitting with the storm outside.

"Oh, good. You're okay." His ghostly shoulders sank with relief as he settled into the nearest kitchen chair.

Sucking a breath through my clenched teeth, I said, "I'm so sorry I worried you. Carl stopped me in the drive-way, wouldn't let me go anywhere because of the storm."

Asher, relaxing as he took in my cozy, safe state, said, "I'm glad he did. It's a mess out there. Misty Drive is flooding where it meets up with Cove Drive, and most of the businesses in the cove are shutting down because of the lightning."

Carl had been right about the flooding. And it sounded like I wouldn't have even been able to get into the station anyway, even if I'd made it into town. I wondered how the canvas yurts were fairing in the storm. Van mentioned he was applying a waterproofer to them a few weeks back, but I didn't know how much that would help in a case like this.

I gazed out the kitchen window, through the rainslashed, blurry glass. The ocean churned and moved like a living being—an angry and scary one at that. Waves larger than any I'd seen yet battered the shore, and what water wasn't wind-whipped white looked slate gray.

"Carl helped me get things ready for the storm," I said absentmindedly, standing on my tiptoes to check on the potted plants we'd pulled under the eves on this side of the house.

"A good thing. Where is he?" Asher asked, scanning the room as if my neighbor might still be here and he hadn't noticed.

I gestured to his house. "He went to take care of his own preparations. It's what he was doing when he saw me driving away, so I interrupted his work."

Asher almost relaxed when he sat up straight and snapped his fingers. "Oh, did you turn off the furnace and then the gas? That basement is so drafty that a big gust of wind can blow the pilot light out and fill the room up with gas. It used to be a problem for your grandmother during storms."

Eyes wide, I shook my head. "I'll go do that really quick."

The entrance to the basement was under the stairs that led up to the house's two bedrooms. I'd only gone down there a few times as it was cold and—as Asher pointed out—drafty. When I'd moved in after Grandma passed away, I'd put some boxes of her stuff down here, not knowing what else to do with it, but also not having time to go through it all.

Those same boxes greeted me as I trotted down the creaky staircase. In order to get access to the furnace, I had to scoot a stack of boxes to the right about half a foot, then

I shimmied in between the stacks to reach the furnace switch.

The large metal contraption shuddered to a halt and the basement quieted. The pilot light burned on, visible through a gap in the furnace's metal. Now I needed to go turn off the gas. Without the hum and whooshing sounds of the furnace, I could hear the wind howl and the rain spatter outside. I wasn't looking forward to going back out there.

A breeze flowed through the space after a particularly loud gust, and I saw why Asher warned about shutting this thing down. I moved quickly, eager to get back upstairs. In my haste, I kicked a stack of framed pictures leaning against the bottom of the boxes. They clattered to the concrete floor after tipping in the other direction.

I sighed and bent down to right them. They weren't pictures Grandma had hanging in her house but ones that she'd stored just like this: propped against something on the floor of the library. I'd moved them down here to make space.

But when I'd moved in, I hadn't known how significant The Pines would be to both myself and Asher. So the black-and-white photograph of my great-grandpa, Richard, with his arm around the shoulders of another man, standing in front of the familiar white farmhouse wouldn't have stood out as anything more than another old photograph. And it definitely wouldn't have given me the full body shivers it did right now as I stared down at it.

This time, my shiver had nothing to do with the drafty basement. My fingers shook too as I brought the framed photograph in for a closer look. My grandmother's father stood in front of a very new version of the house at The Pines, which meant the man his arm wrapped around must've been one of the many Sullivan Mills.

Asher mentioned that his Sullivan, Sully, died before the sizeable house that sat on the property now had been built, which meant this couldn't have been Sully. I squinted at the grainy page, but no matter how much I tried to see the details differently, I couldn't change what this photograph was: Proof my great-grandfather knew Sullivan Mills Junior.

10

Half an hour later, after donning my raincoat once more to run outside and turn off the gas, I'd started a fire in the tearoom fireplace and one in the library stove to combat the furnace being shut down. With the gas off, I wasn't able to use my stove top, but I had electric kettles for the tea shop to heat more water for tea.

I had a fresh cup with me when Asher and I settled into the library.

"Ash," I said carefully, wondering how best to bring this up. "I found something ..."

He lifted his gaze to meet mine, and I chewed on my lip, not quite ready to ask the question. Unfortunately, another few deep breaths and an even more inquisitive stare from Asher didn't help prepare me anymore, so I decided I needed to come out with it. In the months we'd known each other, I'd kept way too many secrets from Asher. Now that everything was out in the open between the two of us, I wasn't about to go down that road again.

"I found a picture downstairs," I said, probably too quickly.

Asher's eyebrows jumped with interest. "A picture of what?"

"My great-grandfather, Richard."

Because there were pictures of the man all over the house, Asher waited, refraining from saying the obvious, "Of course you did."

"He was standing in front of the house at The Pines." I bit out the sentence. Swallowing the rest of my reservations, I added, "And he had his arm around a man I think might be SJ, Sully's son."

Asher's jaw clenched tight, but a banging sound cut his reaction short. At first, I assumed it was the storm, raging outside and sending something smacking up against the siding. When the banging came again, in a very definite "Pop Goes the Weasel" pattern, I realized it must be someone at the door.

I scrambled out of the couch—which took more time than I'd like to admit because its cushions had a tendency to swallow me into them—and padded toward the back door. My thick wool socks slipped slightly as I rounded the corner out of the library and turned into the tearoom.

As I did, Carl walked inside. Actually, he practically blew inside. Dripping and squeaking as he fought with the door, he pressed it closed.

My neighbor growled a greeting. "Sorry to barge in," he said, breathing heavily, "but if I waited out there any longer, I was going to blow away."

Carl's customary form of announcing his arrival was more of a sharp rap before he turned his back on the door and looked out at the ocean while he waited for me to answer. So this barge-right-in version was definitely a change, one I didn't blame him for making in the circumstances.

"No, it's fine. I'm sorry I didn't come right away. I thought it was the storm, knocking something against the house." I rushed toward him, helping him out of that same yellow rain gear.

Soon we had his jacket, rain pants, and hat hanging on a coatrack with a towel underneath to catch the run off.

"Can I get you some tea?" I asked, gesturing to the kitchen.

Carl nodded, rubbing his hands up and down the arms of his cabled wool sweater. I didn't even have to ask what kind of tea he wanted, knowing he preferred the Fishermen's blend.

"I'm in the library if you want to go take a seat." I jerked my head toward the slice of warm yellow light spilling out into the hallway.

"Will do," Carl said, and we parted ways.

A few minutes later, I came in to find my neighbor sitting in Asher's favorite chair with a copy of *The Mysterious Benedict Society* in his lap. He'd kept the bookmark which marked the spot Asher and I were at but had flipped it open to the beginning. He was entranced, his eyebrows pulled tight together as his eyes pored over the text.

I approached with his mug of tea as quietly as possible, setting it on the side table next to him. He still jumped, looking up at me as I did so. Sputtering in surprise, he moved to close the book.

"You know, I planned on skipping this month's club because I didn't think I would enjoy a children's story." He cleared his throat. "But this is quite compelling."

I took my seat on the couch again. I chanced a quick glance at Asher, who winked at me.

My mother, a librarian in Portland, and the person who'd taught me to love books, was helping pick our monthly book club titles. Each one of her picks had not only surprised but delighted the members of the club, and each month we had more people join after hearing their friends rave about the selections they'd read so far. She was also trying to push us out of our normal genres by choosing very different titles each month. So far we'd had a serious literary story, a thriller, an epic fantasy, and now middle-grade fiction.

"Mom's good at what she does," I said, picking up my own, half-gone cup of tea from the table to my left.

I missed her. Usually my mom and I talked every day, but this was her library's big fall fundraiser week, and she'd been working overtime to prepare as well as pulling long days during the event.

I addressed Carl. "There's still time for you to join. We're only halfway through as you can see." I gestured to the bookmark.

Carl glanced up, wrinkling his already creased forehead.

My face went hot as I realized what I'd said. *We*. Asher cleared his throat next to me.

"Uh, me and my mom are staying on pace with each other so neither of us finds stuff out before the other." I hoped he'd buy my excuse.

Carl put down the book, exchanging it for the mug of steaming tea. He closed his eyes and took a sip.

"Your house all good?" I asked.

He nodded but kept sipping as if he couldn't help himself.

I watched him for a moment, waiting for him to say something, explain why he was here, but he didn't.

"Just lonely, then?" I asked carefully, trying not to make it sound like I didn't want his company.

Carl's white eyebrows shot up. "Oh! Sorry, no. I came for a reason." He set down his tea. "You're going to want to shut down the furnace and turn off the gas, so I came to help you with that." He braced himself on the armrests on either side of the chair and pushed himself up.

I held out a hand. "Already did that," I blurted, stopping him.

Carl fell back into the chair, at first appearing relieved that he didn't have to get up, then looking confused. "How'd you know to …?"

"Another of Grandma Helen's notes," I said, adding a click of my tongue at the end to signal it was just luck that I'd read it.

Saved again by those notes, I thought with relief as Carl settled back and picked up his tea once more.

My late grandmother had taken to leaving herself random notes, reminders, and tips around the house in the form of sticky notes. They'd helped me get out of more than one predicament.

"Carl, do you know anything about SJ Mills and my great-grandpa, Richard, who owned this house?" I asked, hoping Carl could help with what I'd found down in the basement.

He perked up, a glint in his blue eyes. "Boy, do I."

My face must've read equal parts interest and dread—Carl's dramatic response made me worried I wasn't ready for the answer.

"They were both great men, of course," Carl said, backtracking as he watched me.

I glanced toward Asher, who appeared doubtful about this. "One of them might have been …" he said.

Carl smiled as if memories ran through his mind. "They

were thick as thieves, those two. I was a young boy at the time, but I still remember that they did everything together."

Just as I relaxed, the light behind Carl's eyes dimmed as if covered by a gray storm cloud.

"That was … until the *whole ordeal*." He strung the two words together as if they would explain themselves. When I only deepened the furrows in my brow, he added, "There are a lot of locals who think SJ stole Richard's company from him." Carl shook his head as if he didn't accept it.

Now Asher gave me the same "see?" look.

All I remembered my grandma telling me about her father was that he was a great fisherman. And obviously he hadn't done too bad, financially, because he had this house. The Victorian on the beach was something I would've never dreamed of affording if it hadn't been left to me when my grandmother passed.

"Stole his company?" I asked, my tone as wobbly as my argument for the Mills family was becoming.

Carl waved his hand in my direction. "You'd have to ask the local historians. I only know hearsay and definitely don't feel comfortable repeating it. And on that note," Carl said, finishing his tea, "I should be going." He held up his mug. "Thank you for the tea. Call if you need anything."

Carl scurried to the door. Squeaks and swearing carried down the hall as Carl scrambled into his wet rain clothes. I stayed put, though, speechless from his confirmation that SJ may not have been the man I'd hoped he was.

Once Carl left, Asher and I sat in silence, letting the information wash over us. I knew Asher didn't believe SJ was a good man, which now felt like a commentary about my great-grandfather. How had the savvy fisherman let himself get swindled out of an entire company?

"Quite the informative night," Asher said at last, his tone strangled by the same discomfort I felt clogging mine.

I could tell he wasn't happy about the information either. This wasn't a game he wanted to win anymore. The reality of its weight now pushing aside any minor argument we'd been having.

"Yeah." I turned to check on the progress of the storm.

Staring at the tumultuous scene outside my window made me feel small, humble, and insignificant. It was the same sentiment I had when I thought about trying to uncover what had happened to Asher a century later.

My mom may be an expert on digging up the answers to history's mysteries, but I didn't have her research skills. And unless I wanted to invite her here to poke around in Van's house with me, this wasn't something she'd be able to solve from her thousands of library databases.

"You should get some sleep," Asher said. His voice startled me, though it was barely more than a whisper. I'd been too lost in my thoughts, in my worries and fears.

I stood. "Yes, you're probably right." I turned my attention to him before I left. "And you'll be okay?"

"I will. One of the greatest perks to not having a body is going out into storms such as this one. It's exhilarating. I'll probably spend the rest of the night out there in the beautiful melee." His eyes wrinkled at the edges as he smiled.

I couldn't help but mimic his expression. And here I'd been thinking my friend was reveling in the cozy warmth inside while the storm raged on outside our windows. He probably would've rather been out there in it all along.

"But never would I choose the company of a storm over you," he added with a wink as if he'd been able to read my exact thoughts.

And with that, he disappeared. I went to bed, thoughts,

worries, and wonderful feelings tumbling through my mind as the storm raged. Before climbing into bed, however, I pulled open the bedroom curtains so I could watch the trees sway and rock in the wind, finding the motion quite soothing.

I needed something soothing, knowing there was a murderer out there somewhere. But the knowledge that Asher was out there too made it feel like I had a guardian watching over me.

Sunlight glinting in through my open bedroom curtains woke me the next morning. I shielded my eyes with my hand as I let them adjust.

Sitting up, I almost couldn't believe what I saw as I peered out the bedroom window. It was beautiful outside, like the storm had blown us back a season and we were right back in the middle of summer. Birds chirped in the trees, and fluffy white clouds dotted a cornflower-blue sky.

I stretched and got up even though it was a good hour before I'd set my alarm.

Asher was sitting in the kitchen when I padded into the room. A yawn overtook me before I could say hello.

"Good morning," he said as my hand covered my open mouth.

"It is. They talk about the calm before the storm, but I've never heard of the peace afterward. Is this usually the case?" I asked, leaning over the sink so I could get a look at the glittering sapphire waves in the calm ocean. "It's as if the storm yesterday didn't happen," I said, shaking my head.

"Not exactly," Asher said in a tone that made me turn

around. He cringed. "You'll change your mind once you see the yard."

A sense of foreboding settled on my shoulders, as if one of the storm swells from last night had crashed right over me. I walked to the back door and peered out at the deck.

Asher was right. Branches littered the deck, plants in the yard were either broken by the wind or appeared to have flattened themselves to the ground in protection. I opened the door and stepped out onto the porch, getting a better look at the side of the house. Some of the potted plants Carl and I had moved under the eaves had still blown over. One had even cracked as it fell. And even though it was sunny, it was downright chilly outside.

Wrinkling my nose, I sighed. "Well, I guess I know what I'm doing with my extra hour."

It took the whole time to clean up the yard. Everything squished and squelched as I picked my way around the property. It all smelled fresh after being doused with rain and ravaged by wind. Even the salty scent of the sea smelled like it had almost been washed right out of the air.

I made a pile of sopping wet branches that had fallen here and there, righted any pots that had fallen over, and fixed the latch on the greenhouse door. Things were much tidier by the time I opened the tea shop.

Every one of my customers that day had their own story about their storm experience. A few people up in the hills had lost power. A tree had fallen on Harriet's deck but had missed her house, thank goodness. Vicki's planter boxes in the windows of the Marina Mug would need replanting, but other than that, all was well.

By the time closing rolled around, I couldn't wait to go downtown and stop by the police station. Asher went ahead, saying he'd wrangle the rest of the local ghosts and see if they'd been able to learn anything from around town.

I got into my car and drove toward town, unimpeded by Carl this time. It was far past time for me to chat with Chief Clemenson about those tea kettles.

11

The debris and damage was not limited to my house, or even Misty Drive. My drive into town was slow as I avoided branches in the road or gawked at the near misses of an entire branch landing next to someone's car or a wind-torn greenhouse. A fair bit of standing water remained at the intersection of Misty Drive and Cove Drive, but nothing my little car had trouble fording.

And the sky was just brilliant.

It almost seemed like the weather was playing a prank on us, trying to make us feel crazy. "What storm? I don't know what you're all complaining about, it's a beautiful fall day."

Downtown, residents of Pebble Cove staggered around in confusion, confirming I wasn't the only one thrown by the sudden change in barometric pressure.

Meow, the town's former mayor and only current feline ghost—to my knowledge—sunned himself by the pier when I parked in the marina lot. He swatted his ghostly tail a few times in a gesture I recognized as an aloof greeting. I approached him and rested my elbows on the boardwalk, pretending to stare out at the cove.

"Good afternoon, former mayor," I said, glancing down at him out of the corner of my eye.

He stayed put. In fact, the only way I knew he'd heard me was that his left ear swiveled in my direction.

"I don't know if you've heard about the young woman killed up at The Pines," I continued, "but I would really appreciate it if you kept your eyes and ears open for anything that might help bring her killer to justice."

Meow couldn't speak, of course, but I was almost positive he understood what I said. I had a handful of evidence proving he could, especially with how he'd helped me solve previous mysteries. And even though his communication was limited to meows, tail flicks, and head nods, he'd given us some of the most important clues in the past. I wasn't silly enough to discount the role he might have in helping us find a killer.

The slow blink that followed told me he'd heard me, but he didn't seem to have anything to add right now.

"Thanks, Meow." I smiled over at him before crossing the street to the station.

The scent of salt sat heavy in the air as usual for our little coastal town, but today it balanced with a mulchy, wet-soil smell. The faintest hint of tar and asphalt hit my nose in waves as the pavement downtown dried in the sunshine.

My boots squeaked slightly as I jogged up the ramp toward the police station. I went to push open the door, but an invisible wall stopped me. I staggered back in confusion. The station door had moved, and slid back into place as I stood there, so it wasn't as if it was locked. I frowned at the lingering chill that came with the push.

About to try again, a figure moved through the door and

blocked my entrance. He was tall, wore an older version of the uniform Chief Clemenson sported, and glowered down at me like I was a bug invading his picnic.

The ghost of former Police Chief Butler, Lois's ex-husband and killer.

It was then that I realized what had happened. "You stopped me," I said, aghast. Although I'd witnessed ghosts using energy to manipulate things in the living world before, I'd never had that energy used against me.

"I will not stand by while you stick your nose in places it doesn't belong." He folded his arms over his transparent body.

From watching Asher, I'd learned using energy took a toll on spirits, manifesting in a dimmed appearance and even foggier senses as well as slower reactions.

"I'm going to give the chief a piece of information he needs." I spat out the statement in as much of a whisper as I could in the state of frustration I was in.

Butler raised his eyebrows in an expression that clearly stated he didn't trust me.

About to argue with him, I noticed a group of locals walking by on the street behind me. I pulled out my phone to make it seem like I wasn't entering the station just yet because I had to make a call.

I didn't dial anyone, but just stuck the phone to my ear and turned to face the ghostly chief once more.

"Look, buddy. I know you'll only be able to keep that up for so long before you run out of energy. Do you really want to test me?" I clenched my teeth as I talked.

I'd waited so long to get to the station, and now that I was here, something new thwarted my progress.

Chief Butler pressed his lips forward as he thought. He

eyed me to see if I told the truth, apparently having assumed I wouldn't know about ghostly energy use.

No surprise there, I thought to myself with an inward snort. The man underestimated all women, especially his ex-wife.

"Maybe I'll just ask Lois to come with me," I said, reminded of how she'd stood up to him in her afterlife.

His smug expression dropped and he backed away.

But before I tried pushing past him and into the station again, the door swung open, and someone stepped out. He nearly knocked me over. Surprised, I dropped my phone from where I'd been holding it up to my ear, pretending to be on a call instead of just arguing with a dead police chief.

In the doorway stood a second surprised police chief, but this one was alive. Startled at my presence, his face set into a grim frown. Then he looked down at my phone and picked it up for me, probably worried the person on the other end of the line would wonder what the loud clattering sound had been.

I opened my mouth to stop him, but he'd already grabbed the phone before I could get a word in. He flipped it over and saw the screen was black.

"Weird, the fall must've hung up my call." I grabbed the phone from him and stuck it in my back pocket. "I'll call her back soon. It was my mother."

I hoped the mention of my mom, with whom Chief Clemenson had gotten along well with during her last few visits, would soften the incredulity lacing his features.

He cleared his throat, taking a step back. "Did you need to come in, Miss Woodmere?" he asked.

I peered at Chief Butler's ghost right behind him, wondering if he'd even let me pass through. "Uh, actually, I wanted to talk with you. Is this a bad time?"

"I'm heading out to get myself some dinner, so if you

don't mind a grumpy, hungry, listening ear, you can walk with me," he said.

Not sure there was a different kind when talking to the chief, I smiled and said, "Not at all." I stepped aside so he could exit the station. Together we walked down the boardwalk.

"So what did you want to tell me?" he asked when we'd walked a few yards and I still hadn't said anything.

"Oh, right. Um, the other night … at the crime scene, I told you the kettle used had been mine, because I had been missing one. But when I got home later that night, I realized I'd just forgotten one at home. The kettle the killer used to hit Clover wasn't one of mine."

The chief studied me. "And it took you three days to tell me this?"

Suddenly worried this might count as impeding an investigation, I stammered, "I—this—there were a lot of … and then the storm." My face flushed with embarrassment. "I tried to tell you when you were at The Pines yesterday, but you gave me that look that said I definitely shouldn't approach."

The chief let out a chuckle, something so out of character, I stopped in the middle of the boardwalk.

He turned around but kept walking, looking over his shoulder to say, "Don't worry, Miss Woodmere. I already knew it wasn't yours because your fingerprints didn't show up anywhere on it."

I jogged forward to catch up to him. "How do you have my fingerprints?"

"Murray's house," was all he had to say.

I'd been involved in a crime scene a few months back. In the aftermath I remembered them taking my prints to make sure they ruled out my prints along with Jolene's who'd also been held at gunpoint alongside me.

"So you're aware the time of death might have been earlier than what I'd originally told you?" I asked.

He puffed out his chest. "Lucky for me, I wasn't basing my entire investigation on the hunch you had. Dr. Ellis also confirmed the time of death as around seven-thirty."

This information spun around me. "Which means it was Cinder."

At this, the chief frowned. "Cinder has an alibi."

I frowned back, knowing he didn't. I thought the chief knew this too. He was the one who came to question him. Had something changed? "But I thought—Meadow said she fell asleep. He was gone when she woke up. I saw him storming past us around seven. He could've gone back to Clover's yurt and finished whatever fight they'd been having after dinner."

The chief sighed. "I'd like to say I'm surprised that you know so much about my investigation, but unfortunately, I'm not." We reached Pizza Cove, one of my favorite local restaurants, and the chief said. "Was that all you needed to tell me, Miss Woodmere?"

"Uh, yeah."

He pointed toward my pocket. "You should probably call your mother back. I'm sure she's worried." With that, he walked into the restaurant.

My fingers curled around the phone. I wished I could call my mom, but I promised myself I wouldn't bug her during this week. I used to work at the library so I knew what a stressful time this was for everyone who worked there. I already felt guilty enough that I wasn't there, wasn't working with her anymore. I wouldn't add to her worry by mentioning my issues.

Instead, I tried to sort out what I'd learned from the chief. The fact that he'd let any of that slip made me think I needed to talk to him when he was hungry more often. I ticked through the facts. So Cinder had an alibi for the time after he left Meadow. But that meant Meadow didn't have an alibi after Cinder had gone, which is when the murder occurred.

Behind me, I heard a familiar voice—well, a familiar meow actually. Could you call a meow a voice?

I turned around, expecting to see the ghostly form of Meow. Instead of his tabby coat and green eyes, I was met with the sleek black coat of Whiskers, his granddaughter, and Pebble Cove's current mayor.

She wore a sparkly collar and a mischievous glimmer in her golden eyes.

"Oh. Hello, Whiskers." I bent down to pet her, reveling in the fact that I could pet her instead of having to pretend she wasn't there like I did with Meow. Other people could see her too.

Her coat was silky smooth, and a purr rumbled out of her throat as she arched up to meet my hand for another scratch. As if she'd gotten what she needed from me, she turned and wandered back toward the marina.

But before she got more than a yard away from me, Whiskers stopped and glanced back at me like she'd said, "You coming?"

I mean, Meow did this kind of thing to me all the time, but I'd assumed it was because he was a spirit. Whiskers might simply lead me toward food she wanted me to feed her or something else more typically catlike. I followed because … why not?

Whisker's little feet made no noise as she padded in front of me. The contrast between her and my squeaky boots made me feel like an elephant stomping behind the dainty, silent creature. She held her black tail high, like a little flag waving, showing me where to go.

And just as quickly as she'd taken off, the mayor stopped, sitting on her haunches, and staring ahead. I almost didn't halt in time and had to jump over her so I wouldn't step on her. That was another way she differed from Meow, who I would've merely passed through.

"Yeah, I'm downtown. I don't know, it's like they only sell fish and, like, nets down here." The voice pulled my attention from where I'd been looking down at the mayor.

Meadow was on the phone, standing at the entrance to Jolene's tea shop. The exact person I needed to talk to.

"I think there's a tea room if you're okay with that," she said in a snotty tone that made it sound like she wasn't. "Okay, I'll see you there in fifteen minutes. That's okay. I can get something while I wait." She hung up the call and started toward Jolene's shop.

I could've followed her, but I froze. If Meadow was the killer, she wouldn't tell me. I needed to figure it out on my own. Her yurt and the intriguing plastic bin of Polaroids in the corner came to mind. Maybe I could find something in there.

She was meeting someone from the sounds of it. And no matter how quickly the meeting went, she would be waiting for at least fifteen minutes. Which gave me time to go up to The Pines.

I needed to find out the truth about Meadow once and for all.

12

My foot eased down onto the brake as I felt my car lean a little too much to the left around a hairpin-like turn. That corrected the motion, and I pressed down on the accelerator again, zooming uphill toward The Pines.

I'd have to watch that next corner, though. I wouldn't be able to find out any information about Meadow if my car careened off the cliffs and into the ocean. I took the next few at a slower pace.

The final bend came into view and I slowed the car. Other than concentrating on staying on the road, I'd also spent the last five minutes coming up with a plan of how to get into Meadow's yurt without bringing too much attention to myself. Unfortunately, with the parking lot right next to the main house, I couldn't see that happening.

But that was when the trail Asher had shown me came to mind. It came up right next to that hollow trunk—and, more importantly—Meadow's yurt. I could walk up and slip into Meadow's place unnoticed.

Pulling off onto the shoulder should've been no big deal.

People did it all the time, trying to get a peek of the sea through the sparse pines here along the cliff's edge.

But I'd parked here before.

When I'd first suspected Althea, the former owner of The Pines, of being the one responsible for my grandmother's death. The reality that I'd stopped here to sneak up and investigate another potential murderer made the whole situation all the more chilling.

And if I wasn't on a strict time line, I might've stopped to contemplate these feelings a little longer. But I needed to get moving before Meadow came back. More storm clouds rolled in, covering the sun and the peaceful blue sky. If it rained again, it might flush everyone out from downtown, sending them back up here.

I stepped out of my car, locking it behind me. The old abandoned cannery building was a concrete skeleton in the woods below the cliff. I turned my back on it and turned into the woods. I only had to fight with the underbrush and branches for a few yards before locating the trail Asher and his friends must've used. I wasn't sure if the footpath was still intact because other people had used it since or if it had become something of a wildlife pathway, but I welcomed the reprieve from sticks and leaves slapping me in the face as well as a bit of direction.

Birds chirped, unseen in the quiet forest. The only other sound was the distant crash of waves. It sounded like the ocean was gearing up for a second round of this storm along with the sky.

Passing by the hollowed-out trunk, I paused at the edge of the yurt-dotted field for a moment, assessing the situation. A few people milled about in the community garden, but it was fairly quiet. Those who were outside kept glancing up at the foreboding cloud above as if it were a person following them too closely down a dark alleyway.

I skirted around the back of Meadow's yurt, running my fingers along the canvas material. The fabric flaps that made up her doorway weren't drawn open like the last time I'd visited, but they weren't tied shut either, so I slipped inside. This was even better because the closed flaps hid the fact that I was inside from anyone passing by or who might glance out from the main house.

Inside was surprisingly cozy given there were no insulated walls or a sturdy door to keep out the elements. I located a small cordless heater in the middle of the space and realized that would be a necessity as we moved from fall into winter. Her twin-sized bed had been neatly made with that floral quilt brightening up the space. Besides a few large potted plants and a dresser, there was a small desk in one corner.

I bypassed all of it for the large bin of pictures sitting along the side of the tent. There had to be a hundred Polaroids tossed into the container. I pulled my sleeves over my hands to cover my fingerprints and sweep over the pictures to move the ones on top aside. Unlike the pictures pinned to the board hanging from the tent side—which were of a diverse mix of people—those in the bin were predominantly of two people.

Meadow and Clover.

Using my covered thumb to dig deeper into the bin of pictures, I found proof of a Halloween party, time spent in coffee houses, adventures around Portland, the usual stuff friends might do.

But about halfway down into the bin, one picture made me freeze. My heartbeat ratcheted up so much I could hear it pounding loudly. One of the Polaroids had been written on with a sharpie.

The word LIAR was scrawled across Clover's face.

In fact, many of the pictures surrounding and below that one had the same word written across them.

A quick check of my surroundings told me that the sound of rain splattering on the canvas of the surrounding yurt had joined the pounding in my ears. The violence of the drops and the din they made, caused me to wonder if I was safe inside here.

The next picture that caught my eye convinced me I wasn't safe, but not because of the weather.

Meadow stood in the forefront, hair braided into a plait that lay over one shoulder as she posed in what looked like a Mother Nature Halloween costume. What caught my attention was the couple in the background. Clover and Van. And they were kissing.

The crunch of footsteps along the pathway near the yurt made me jump.

How could she be back so soon? I wondered in frustration.

But the continued sound of the rain outside reminded me that Meadow could've cut her meeting short because of the weather. Panic engulfed me. Meadow had been mad enough at Clover about something that she'd ruined pictures of them together. Had she been mad enough to kill?

And then there was the fact that Van, dressed as Dr. Alan Grant from *Jurassic Park*, had his lips on Clover dressed as Dr. Ellie Sattler. Van never mentioned he and Clover had a past. Then again, I hadn't ever asked. Maybe he'd told all of this to the police, and I was making something out of nothing.

The footsteps grew louder and brought me out of my panicky thoughts and into my panicky present situation. I needed to get out of here before Meadow found me snooping around.

The only way out of this thing was through the front doorway. And by the closeness of the footsteps, there was no way I would be able to sneak out unseen. I glanced at the photographs I still held in my hand—the one with Clover and Van kissing and one of the LIAR pictures—and stuffed them into my jacket pocket. I stood as the footsteps grew louder; I sat on Meadow's bed and tried to appear like I was innocently waiting for her.

Waiting for Clover's possible murderer.

So when Van stuck his head through the opening in the tent moments later, I about cried in relief. The picture in my pocket stopped me from letting my guard down completely, but I was still much happier to see him than Meadow.

His gaze settled on me, a mild worry wrinkling the edges. He blinked as he did a double take. "Oh, Rosemary. What—how'd …?" His questions petered out and he wrinkled his forehead.

I sucked in a breath, unsure how to explain my presence in Meadow's yurt or the fact that my car wasn't in the parking lot. Luckily, just as I opened my mouth to stumble through a chain of probably incoherent lies, thunder rolled overhead like someone was banging giant sheet pans above the yurt.

"Where's Meadow?" he asked. "The lightning is starting up again. I'm gathering everyone inside the farmhouse. Come on." Van grabbed onto my wrist, pulling me with him.

There was something about how tightly Van's hand clasped around my wrist that made me want to run away from him, even if it meant being at the mercy of the storm.

I lined up the words to tell Van my car was right down

on the road and I would be fine driving home when the rain began falling in sheets. The evening light had all but vanished, covered by an ashy cloud, and I wondered if I would even be able to see in the gloom. We dashed out from the cover of the yurt and joined the other residents running across the community lawn toward the large white farmhouse.

Inside, Van whipped off his rain jacket and hung it on a hook near the back door. A small puddle formed from the rain slicking off it. I kept mine on, not wanting to part from the incriminating photographs tucked in the pocket inside the liner. When someone looked at me in question, I squeezed my shoulders up to my ears, motioning that I was too cold to take off the jacket. The two dozen people staying in the yurts followed Van's lead, though, peeling off their soaked rain jackets and making their own puddles inside.

The combination of that noise with the squeak of wet shoes on the wooden floor of the kitchen almost rivaled the din happening outside. Almost. Another round of lightning flashed above the house, followed closely by what sounded like an entire fleet of garbage trucks dropping dumpsters simultaneously. It was almost pitch black outside, feeling like midnight instead of just after dinnertime.

People weren't huddled together in fear, but there was a collective unease, an eeriness hanging in the air almost as palpable as the humidity. I glanced around, searching for Meadow, unsure if she'd been able to make it back from downtown before the storm hit.

But it didn't matter. Seconds later, the lights flickered once, twice, and then pitched the room into darkness.

13

Inside the kitchen of The Pines farmhouse, the room felt charged with as much electricity as the storm held outside.

Van walked over to the sink and turned on an electric lantern. He pulled out a pack of matches as if it were an everyday occurrence to lose power. And maybe it was this far out of town. The candles—both the tall tapered kind and short votives—lined up along the windowsill told me it had definitely happened recently. He got to work lighting candles, and soon there were glimmers of light within the shadows.

The kitchen was a huge, industrial space that not only held large stainless steel workspaces and racks but also had enough room for a smaller table and stools pushed up against the stainless steel workspaces. So even with over twenty of us crammed inside, it wasn't too bad.

As if the power had turned off outside too, an inky blanket covered the sky. What is it about storms that come at night that makes them even more ominous? Another rumble shook the old house, and sheets of rain were visible in the light that split the sky just a mile or so south over Desperation Cliff.

"How about we put on some water for tea?" Van said, breaking everyone's concentration on the storm.

He'd held onto the matches after lighting the candles and used one to light the gas stove. Grabbing a kettle from the stove top to fill it, he looked at me.

"I have a bag of your Home blend, Rosemary. Should I make a pot or two of that?" he asked as the flames on the gas stove top licked around the edges of the teapot, and it clicked in that oh so comforting way.

I nodded. The spicy, cinnamon-flavored Home blend was my absolute favorite of my grandmother's custom blends. The act of making tea made me long to be in my home with Asher, cozy with blankets and books. Instead, I was here in a house I had less than pleasant memories of, with a possible murderer.

I didn't see Meadow or Cinder anywhere in the sparse light provided by the flickering candles and Van's lantern. My fingers tapped on the stainless steel counter in my nervousness, so I said, "I'd be happy to make it."

Really, I was glad for the distraction.

Van seemed pleased and handed over the bag of tea leaves. Cinder walked in at that moment. I had to remind myself that he had an alibi. He wasn't Clover's killer.

Through the open door, something caught Van's eye because he said, "Actually, Cinder, don't take off your coat. I'm going to need your help to grab more wood for the fireplace." He walked over to where Cinder stood, dripping wet by the back door, and pulled on his own jacket.

They left, and I busied myself with the tea-making process.

At first, the group was quiet, listening in for the timing

between the thunder and the flashes of lightning. But after a few minutes, they whispered in groups.

Meadow's name caught my ear, but I kept my head down and focused on the tea preparation.

"Has anyone seen her?" a young woman asked the group in a whisper. She scanned the crowd, but everyone shook their heads.

"I think I saw her going into town," a man about my age said.

While this answered the question about where she'd gone, this didn't seem to alleviate any of the obvious worry written on the different residents' faces. In fact, this piece of information only darkened the shadows of doubt already present in their expressions.

"Do you think they called her down to the station?" someone whispered as others began exchanging stories about the worst storm they'd been through in their lives.

I focused in on the conversation about Meadow.

The man who'd asked stared at the woman next to him. She shrugged. "It's possible. I mean, she was the one who found Clover. Isn't that usually something?"

Speaking from experience as someone who'd found a body I definitely hadn't killed, I hated that stereotype. But I couldn't help but agree with the woman in this circumstance. Though my suspicion stemmed more from the evidence of anger scrawled across the photographs stuffed in my jacket pocket at that moment as well as her lack of an alibi.

Cinder and Van stomped back inside. Everyone quieted. I wasn't sure if it was more for Cinder or Van. The picture of Van kissing Clover and the way he'd grabbed me in the tent both sat like a cold, wet shirt against my skin.

The tea was ready, and I poured out mugs for each

person who came forward. Van went off to build a fire in the living room and the rest of the residents followed. Soon I was alone in the kitchen. Having been a rather unpleasant place for me during the last experience I'd had in this house, I headed elsewhere.

Though I'd never seen a library in my travels through the house, a place like this had to have one. I mean, in my opinion, every house ought to have one, but an old manor like this definitely would unless it had been converted into something else.

I grabbed a candle before leaving the kitchen. Candlelight spilled into the dark hallway from the living room. Even though I could hear the fire crackling inside, I also heard voices, which meant that was where the majority of the guests had disappeared to. I really didn't want to deal with awkward silences and whispered rumors right now. I continued past, toward the back of the house.

The candle in my hand made shadows dance across the walls. The old wooden floors creaked under my feet, betraying my presence this far down the hallway.

I opened the first door but only found a bathroom. The next one was a closet. The other door to my right led down into the basement, something I knew from experience, so that meant my last hope was the last door on the right.

Even though it was dark out because of the dense cloud cover from the storm, I could see the outline of shelves and, most importantly, the spines of books in what little light spilled inside from the flame of my candle. A smile pulled at the corners of my mouth. Scents of leather and dust mingled in the cool space.

The door creaked about halfway closed behind me, but it didn't shut. Not loving the idea of being shut inside a room alone, I let it remain open. The books called to me.

But as much as the sight of shelves full of books made me feel more at home, I'd been wrong. This was nothing like my library.

Other than the absence of a fire, there was a chill in the air. It was the exact chill I felt when Asher or one of the other spirits touched me, or I accidentally walked through them. I glanced around, moving the flame with me.

There was no one else in here with me.

I sighed and turned my head to the side as I approached the shelf. Every reader knows this position, where you tilt your head toward your shoulder so you can read the titles along the spines as you walk next to the shelves. This collection was quite well rounded. I recognized many classics in leather bindings and sporting gilt pages and titles. But there were modern best sellers as well. Among them was also a slew of books I knew weren't close to best sellers, but that I had enjoyed reading very much.

And then there was one that caught my eye. *Mills Family History*.

Eyes wide, I pulled that volume from the shelf and opened it, gazing down at its pages in the flickering candlelight. It was one of those photo books anyone can make on the internet, but it held more text than I was used to seeing.

My mission to figure out why or how Sullivan Mills the First had killed Asher came crashing back onto my shoulders. I'd gotten distracted with Clover's death and the clues I'd uncovered about that, but this was the mystery that really meant something to me—and the one no one but Asher and I were looking into. I needed to let the chief focus on Clover's death while I kept my focus on Asher's.

I'm not sure what I expected to find inside the pages of the family history. Surely the author, Sullivan Mills the

Third—Van's late father—wouldn't include a section all about deadly feuds. Flipping through it, I found I was right.

What the book included was glorified paragraphs about the first Sullivan Mills and how he'd paved the way for the family's fortunes. I lifted an eyebrow, remembering Asher say that both Sully and Abigail had died poor. Their son, SJ, had been the one to make the family fortune and build the impressive house I stood in right now. So how could Sully take credit for that?

Reading further, I felt the animosity Sullivan the Third—or Ivan, as Van had told me his father went by—felt for his father. Apparently, even though SJ made the lion's share of the family fortune, he was quite generous, giving much of what he earned to charities and paying his workers a larger than average salary. Ivan wrote about this charity diplomatically, but it was something about his word choice, the lack of flowery, worshiping vocabulary he'd used when describing his grandfather showed his distaste for the man's philanthropy.

Of course, that charity meant nothing if SJ had stolen the company from my great-grandfather in the first place.

After turning to a page that held the same black-and-white photograph I had of Richard and SJ standing in front of the house, I closed the book. A quick scan of Ivan's version of the story mentioned nothing but a *joint shipping company* Richard and SJ ran together. No luck finding any further truths there.

Putting the history book back, I continued reading titles along the shelf. A history of the family wouldn't give me what I needed. Maybe a picture album could help. I found something even better a moment later. A hardback journal with the word *Diary* inscribed along the spine caught my eye.

But just as I moved to pluck it off the shelf, the door into the library creaked behind me.

I only glimpsed Van's face coming toward me in the flicker of my candle before he leaned forward and blew out the flame.

14

I jumped back, letting out a strangled screech.

Van stood next to me. His eyes widened.

"Rosemary, calm down. I'm sorry. It's just me." He held up his hands, one of which held a flashlight.

Yeah, that's what I'm worried about, I thought to myself.

My gaze flicked between his face and the light. I hoped all of my questions about why he'd blown out my candle were written on my face because I was too surprised to verbalize them.

"I didn't want you to singe any of the books." He pointed to the shelf in front of me. "You were getting close there with the flame. Sorry, I didn't realize it would scare you so much." He watched me take in his explanation as if he would gauge his next words on how I accepted these.

Maybe I *had* been getting close to the books. It was likely I'd forgotten that the light I held was a flame, and not a flashlight.

I exhaled the rest of my worries. "The storm has me a little jumpy, I guess."

Van returned to his normal easy, laid-back posture almost instantly. "This is a great room, isn't it?" he asked.

"Libraries are usually my favorite place in a house," I said in lieu of a direct answer about this library in particular.

Even with the light of Van's flashlight, I still felt clammy and chilled, like something wasn't right about this space. There was also something not right about how close Van stood to me. I inched away, my attention lingering on the diary sitting in front of me on the shelf. I wished I could grab it without Van noticing.

"This room is definitely my favorite here," he said. "I've learned so much about my family from the books inside this library." He studied the space, then settled into one of the old wingback chairs facing the shelves.

I followed suit, sitting in the other chair and setting my extinguished candle on the side table in between us. Pulling a match from his pocket, he relit my candle and clicked off the flashlight. As much as my instincts told me to run away from him, the promise of getting information about his family was too enticing to pass up.

"I saw the family history your dad wrote," I said conversationally, trying to cover up my eagerness. "Is that what you've been reading?"

Van scoffed, "My dad didn't write that. That man couldn't find a thing in the world he couldn't hire out. He hired someone to look up that history for him and took the credit, as usual." Van's eyebrows lifted in exasperation. "Hiring people to do his dirty work was how my father operated. No, that family history is a joke. Even if he didn't write it, he still controlled what went in and what didn't. My father hated his father, Sullivan Junior," Van said, agitation tightening his tone. "He spent my whole life complaining about the man and how he made terrible business decisions, how he lead with his heart instead of his brain."

Trying hard to keep the disappointment from my features, I nodded along. I was supposed to be digging for information about Sully and his feud with Asher, not SJ. Still, I wasn't going to turn away information about SJ either, knowing now what I did about the possible scandal between him and my great-grandfather.

The candlelight sent shadows dancing through the mostly unlit room, making me feel like we weren't alone in here. I couldn't tell if it was comforting or disturbing.

"SJ was so much more than my father ever let us believe. He died when we were very young, so all Liv and I had to go by was what our dad told us about the man," Van continued.

I could relate somewhat, having lost my grandfather, Helen's husband, as well as both of my mom's parents, young.

"It's like finding out I'm not alone in this family," Van said with a smile. His eyes widened with worry as he must've heard how that sounded. "Liv's great, but she's definitely our father's daughter when it comes to the business. It's why Dad left her in charge of everything when he passed away."

"How did your dad die?" I asked before considering it might be a rude question. "Sorry." I shook my head. "You don't have to answer that."

Van held up a hand. "No worries. Dad was seventy-five this year. He'd had a heart problem for years after not taking care of himself and not managing his stress. The doctors said it got to be too much for his heart." While Van appeared sad as he talked, there was a note of detachment in his tone.

My mom was only in her fifties, so Van's dad must've been much older when he and Liv were born.

"Sorry, back to SJ. What else did you admire about him?" I asked, wondering how to bring up the business rumor. Carl seemed to doubt the story, and this was becoming yet another mystery I wanted to solve.

Van looked up as if he literally had the man on a pedestal in his mind's eye. "He was so … generous. Despite what my dad believed, he was the smartest business man I've ever studied." Van looked around. "And he built this house with his own two hands, so that's impressive. Well, he and his best friend built it together."

I tipped my head to one side. "His best friend? Who was that?" I was terrible at lying, so I hoped I didn't have to keep up the ruse I didn't know the best friend was my great-grandfather, too long.

Van's face lit up. "A local guy named Richard Fuller."

"That's my great-grandpa," I said, trying to sound shocked. Letting him go on felt too much like lying. "Now that you mention it, I think I found a picture of them standing in front of this house," I added, hoping sharing some information of my own would help Van open up.

"From what SJ wrote about their friendship, it sounds like one of those connections that changes each person for the better, you know?" Van shook his head like he couldn't imagine such a relationship.

I nodded. I could.

Asher was that person for me. His friendship hadn't made me a different person, just the best version of myself. But from the rumors circulating around town about SJ and Richard, I wasn't sure Van was right about their friendship.

Cursing myself for pretending not to know anything about SJ, I wondered how I could bring up the allegations without raising questions. I also didn't know how good of an idea it was to accuse Van's grandpa of being a swindler after he'd just gone on about how much he looked up to the man.

"I'm glad to hear that my great-grandpa had such a good friend. I think he needed it after everything he went through," I said.

Van's eyebrows rose with interest. "What did he go through?"

"I heard someone stole his company from him." I pushed the words forward before I chickened out.

Understanding dawned on Van's features, but the effect was almost sinister in the candlelight. "A common misconception." He cleared his throat. "I found—"

But I didn't hear the rest of what he said because an older man came blundering into the room.

"I stole nothing!" he shouted, raising a finger in the air.

Even without having seen a picture of him as a younger man, I would've known it was SJ's ghost: that he floated through the door on his way into the room also made it pretty clear.

Tempering my reaction so Van wouldn't think I was crazy, I turned my attention back to the younger—and living—Mills.

"... there are even financial records that show Richard sold the company to SJ, and not for a small amount," Van continued.

I blinked, SJ's ghostly entrance having caused me to miss a major part of that, it seemed. "Wait. What?" I asked.

Van shrugged. "SJ left behind financial books for the company. He managed the company for Richard for a decade before buying it from him."

"Exactly," SJ said, standing behind Van as if he was content to let his grandson fight his battles for him.

"Oh," I said, resisting the urge to check with SJ for clarification. Placing a hand on my forehead, I sighed. "Would you mind getting me a glass of water? I'm feeling a little light-headed. Maybe it's the smoke from the candle," I suggested lamely, hearing immediately how flimsy that sounded.

If Van thought it was a poor excuse, he didn't let on. He got up to leave. Once the door was shut and his footsteps receded down the hallway, I turned to SJ who was pacing at the other end of the room, looking like he might leave as well.

"SJ," I said carefully, not sure why I worried about scaring a ghost. "I can see you, and hear you, but Van doesn't know that."

The spirit whirled around, meeting my eyes with his piercing blue gaze. The intensity in his features scared me, and I worried he would be the first angry ghost I'd met. Then his mouth broke into an enormous grin.

"A medium. How delightful. I never thought I'd meet one of your kind." He came toward me, his legs moving like he was walking this time instead of floating around as he'd been before.

The preference between floating and walking seemed completely situational, or that had been the case with the spirits I'd met so far. I'd experienced all of them do both at different times.

As much as I would've loved to chat about my gift more, I needed to get information before Van returned. "Is he telling the truth? You didn't steal my great-grandpa's company from him?"

His face lit up. "Richard's great-granddaughter? What a treat. I miss that old bugger." Nostalgia took over, and I could tell he was losing his focus.

"Sir, focus. We don't have much time." I snapped my fingers.

"Apologies. Yes, what Van said is very much true. I'm embarrassed that anyone around here would think otherwise. Richard and I were friends until the end. When he inherited that shipping business from his father, it was during the Great Depression. Richard, you see, was one of those fishermen who dried up and got salty if he spent too much time away from the sea. And as much as he tried to stick it out and run the company for the sake of the employees, it killed him to be away from his ship." SJ settled into a chair near me.

And though I found this all profoundly interesting, I knew we were running out of time. SJ seemed to sense my urgency because he sat up a little straighter and picked up the pace of his story.

"I told Richard I would work with him, taking over the managing side of the company. I'd been laid off of my job after the crash, and while I wasn't desperate for money yet, I needed something to keep me interested. Together, Richard and I saved that failing company and even expanded our workforce after a few years. After ten years, he asked if I wanted to buy the company from him, saying he was proud of what we'd accomplished, but was done. I insisted on paying slightly more than his valuation and Richard bought himself a new boat. Everyone was happy."

"That's so much better than the version I heard," I said through a sigh. "I'm glad he had a friend like you."

SJ smiled. "Richard was the best friend I ever had. And even though I went a lot earlier than him, we had many marvelous years together."

His mention of death felt like a quick slap to the face. I hadn't even considered the fact that SJ's spirit was still here.

Why hadn't he moved on? I felt the question rise in my throat. What unfinished business did he have?

Just like Asher, SJ seemed to be able to read my thoughts.

"I don't know why I'm still here," he whispered. "I thought it was my Ivan, that I needed to watch over him and make sure he didn't ruin his life with selfish pursuits. But it turns out I wasn't successful with that. The poor boy was angry and stubborn until the day he died." SJ shrugged. "But Ivan's gone now, and I'm still here. So I must be here for another reason."

"There was nothing strange about your death, then? No possibility you were harmed and you are unaware?" I frowned.

"No," he said. "I had cancer. It had been with me a long time, had taken a huge toll on my body and my family. In the end, I almost welcomed death, so I wouldn't have to see my loved ones suffer anymore. I think it's part of the reason Ivan held me at such a distance. He knew early in his life that I would not be around for the whole of it. Maybe it was easier for him to push me away. The fact that I lived to see him become a father in his own right surprised us all, I think."

Sadness filled me at the story, but it was matched with the warmth of SJ's kind nature and understanding. The man was a delight to talk with. Which made it even harder when Van came back with my water.

"Thank you so much," I said as I took the glass from Van, but looked at SJ.

Van sat down across from me again. "You're welcome." He closed his eyes for a moment. "It's so much more relaxing back here than with all of them." Eyes flashing open, he added, "I like the residents; don't get me wrong."

I took a long sip of the water. "I understand. I prefer quiet gatherings too."

Something about Van's concern and the way he worried about how people saw him told me his worst nightmare would be someone thinking of him as cruel or unfeeling like his father. Which just didn't sound like a killer to me.

The photographs in my pocket, however, reminded me of the kiss between him and Clover, the victim in this whole mess.

Unsure how to bring something like this up, I reverted to the question I'd asked him before. "So you said you knew Cinder before he came here. Is there anyone else?"

Van ran his hand along the side of his face. "Yeah, I went to college with Jenny and Nick."

I sat there for a moment, not sure who Jenny or Nick were, waiting for him to say he knew Clover.

"What about Clover?" I asked when he said nothing more. "Did you know her before all of this?"

Van shook his head sadly. "No. I met her when she moved here. I wish I'd been able to get to know her better, though."

My stomach dropped. Asher might actually be right about Van being the killer.

15

Van had lied to me. I had the photograph in my pocket to prove it. The sudden reality that I might be sitting with a murderer sank in, making me awkward as all get out. The next few minutes dragged by as I tried to ask about how he'd met Jenny and Nick—if he even knew them, given his propensity for lying.

I was about to make up an excuse to leave when the door to the library slammed open.

"Van, we need you. It's Cinder." One of the yurt dwellers raced forward, his body tense and expression hard.

Van glanced up in apology before chasing after the man.

Sighing in relief, I let myself relax now that I was alone.

"Has he done something?" SJ's voice reminded me I wasn't.

I looked at the ghost for a few moments, trying to think of what to say. Van definitely thought the world of SJ, and by the way he looked at his grandson, it seemed SJ shared the feeling. I didn't want to accuse Van of murder after one lie.

"SJ, I don't know yet." The sadness in my tone lowered my shoulders and registered on SJ's ghostly face.

This was his house, one he helped build with his own hands, so the man looked like he was as solid as me or any of the books the surrounding shelves held. But he looked like he belonged on the set of a Sinatra film instead of in this contemporary library. His white hair was swiped to one side like Van's.

At least he'd made it to an age where he had white hair, I thought with a glimmer of optimism.

"You didn't happen to see what happened to the young woman who died the other day?" I asked, hope rising in my heart.

SJ shook his head before my hopes could get too high. "I took a walk in the woods that night. I'm so sorry."

I tried to tamp down my disappointment. Leave it to me to befriend every ghost who loves to take solitary walks in the woods or on the beach. For once, I'd love for one spirit I communicate with to say, "Oh, I saw that. Yeah, it was so and so who killed that person, without a doubt."

"That's okay," I said. Squinting as I remembered the other murder I was investigating, I added, "Any chance there's anything in this house that would help me get to know your father better?"

SJ's face clouded over faster than the sky had with this second storm. I was glad I didn't come right out and ask if he thought his father could be a murderer. SJ glanced over at the family history book I'd been looking through earlier.

"Nothing that will tell you the truth." He snorted.

I'd feared as much.

"Probably the closest thing would be my mother's journal." He motioned over to the bookshelf.

Right. The diary. I'd almost forgotten about it. Following SJ over to the shelf, it surprised me when his ghostly finger indicated a completely different book than the one I'd been eyeing before. While I'd guessed it would be the gilt-edged, fancy journal that had the word printed on the spine, the volume SJ pointed to was made of cracked, dingy leather.

"My mother was a writer her whole life. It's how she processed things. I never had the guts to read that, wasn't sure what I'd find inside its pages. It seemed too personal. But I also didn't have the heart to throw it away. You can take it."

I paused. "You sure?"

"It's my house, isn't it?" He let out a booming laugh that I could swear I felt even though he wasn't physically here with me.

I plucked the thing off the shelf, sticking it in my pocket along with the photographs. "I'll return it. I promise."

From the front of the house, the sound of the front door opening and closing multiple times caught my attention. Footsteps rang through the hallway. Glancing outside, I confirmed the rain had let up to a general drizzle instead of the pouring it was doing earlier. Misty droplets glittered in the dark as they fell. The sun must've fully set behind the dark clouds while we'd been hunkered down inside during the storm.

"We should probably see what the commotion is." SJ sent me a grin that reminded me of the conspiratorial kind my father used when he was thinking up a prank we could play on my mother.

Letting me exit first, SJ followed me down the hall and through the front door of the farmhouse. My candle's flame flickered as I walked, and I joined the other flames and flashlights gathered outside. From the porch steps I could see the parking lot easily thanks to a large solar floodlight mounted on the exterior of the house. The rest of the community members, along with Van, stood in a huddle at the edge of the parking lot watching Cinder throw bags into his Prius.

Whispers floated back to where SJ and I stood behind them.

"Did you see the picture?"

"Yes, I can't believe it."

"I seriously feel sick to my stomach."

"There's no way he can come back from this."

My mind reeled. The chief had cleared Cinder. He'd said his alibi was solid. Was there new information? And if so, why were they letting him leave?

"What's going on?" I asked, approaching the group. "Is he leaving?"

Could he even do that in the middle of an investigation?

People glanced back at me, their eyes shining with a light only good gossip elicited.

"You'll never believe it," one woman whispered to me. Then she did some kind of double take as she realized I wasn't one of the residents. She must've decided I was still worth telling because she said, "Someone recognized him and took a picture of him in another town the night of the murder, and the police confirmed it with the video footage in the restaurant, so he's off the hook."

"Then why does he seem so angry?" I asked, observing him as he bullied a duffle bag into his trunk like it owed him money.

The woman's eyes widened. "He was in a fast-food restaurant."

I shrugged.

The expression of pure incredulity the woman shot me after I said that told me I should be more shocked. Then I remembered Van telling me that Cinder was a famous vegan blogger and YouTuber.

She saw the understanding dawn on my features. "He was eating a burger. Some double-stacked monstrosity." She shuddered as if ground beef was the worst thing in the world.

"Wow," I said, but anything else felt crass as Cinder slammed his car door and peeled out of the parking lot in his Prius.

Van put up his hands. "Now, everyone please remember that this place is all about peace and community. Even though Cinder may have had a lapse with his culinary standards, that doesn't mean we need to be the ones to spread the gossip."

The people gathered around nodded, but I could see some of them slip their fingers into their pockets, fingers itching to let someone over the internet know about this scandal. It was the first time I'd seen any of them with their devices, actually, part of the community's goal being a life untethered from technology—as Van had once explained to me. They scattered, and I could've sworn I heard the ping of a dozen messages as they each texted everyone they knew.

Van turned to me, sighing. "Well, hopefully that's the last drama we'll have for a while."

"Other than figuring out who killed Clover, of course," I said, watching him. The flame on my candle sizzled out in the misty rain as I stepped forward.

"Right. Yes, of course." His cheeks turned red even

though the windchill dropped by the moment, and the rain picked up again.

I stuck my candle-free hand inside the outside pockets of my rain jacket, letting my thumb trace the diary and photographs sitting in the inside pocket. I looked up at the sky, regretting the action when a raindrop plopped right onto the corner of my eye.

"Well, I think I might take off," I said to Van, blinking at the excess moisture in my eye and handing him the candle.

He frowned as he took the candle. "You sure? The rain's still bad. And it's dark out."

I waved as I walked toward the driveway. "Positive. A little rain doesn't scare me."

What scared me were murderers trying to cover their evil deeds. I picked up the pace, hoping Van didn't think too much about how my car wasn't in the parking lot and I was running down the road. I pulled out my phone and turned on my flashlight, pointing it ahead of me.

I heard Van yell something after me, but didn't turn around to figure out what it was. Instead, I picked up a jog as I rounded the first corner. Tires squealed and my heart jumped into my throat.

A shiny black Tesla screeched to a halt where it had swerved on its way up to The Pines. I cringed and waved in apology, pointing my flashlight at the ground so I didn't blind the driver as much as the car's headlights had momentarily blinded me. I hadn't heard it coming since it was electric, and my pounding heart must've covered the sound of its tires. The back window motor hummed as the tinted sheet of glass disappeared down into the door. Meadow's face poked out from the back seat, a string of questions written in her expression.

But I didn't even give her the chance to say anything. Instead, I started jogging again.

Van had obviously lied about knowing Clover, and Meadow had been angry enough with her to deface a bunch of pictures. I couldn't tell who was the guilty party, but I knew one thing: I needed to get away from The Pines.

16

My car had never looked so wonderful. I got in and peeled out, down the hill. The rain pelted the windshield faster than the wipers could get rid of it as I neared the end of the hill coming down from The Pines.

Thoughts of fires, tea, blankets, and my best friend called me home. But the pictures I had in my pocket were too much to let go. This wasn't like the kettle. This was something Chief Clemenson might not be aware of.

I steered the car left toward town. But before I drove a foot away from the stop sign, it was as if I got a flash forward, a glimpse into the future. I could see the chief with his fingers pressed tight to his forehead, sighing at me and asking me—sarcastically, of course—how I expected him to use evidence that I'd stolen from Meadow's yurt against her and Van.

Wrinkling my nose, I changed my mind and turned right, toward home instead. It was late, and I didn't know if the chief would even be at the station right now. Maybe if I ran these clues by Asher, we could figure out a way to lead the chief to the same clues, legally, and I could let him know in the morning.

As I drove closer to Tea by the Sea, SJ's comments about best friends made a warmth radiate through me, helping the chilly night seem less like it had gotten into my bones.

My house was a warm hug when I entered. Well, not *warm* exactly because I'd left the gas off, and the fires I'd made for the customers earlier today had long burned out. But it was home, nonetheless. Soft yellow light spilled from the tearoom down the hall.

"Hello. I'm home," I called as I hung my purse on the hook in the hallway closet off limits to customers.

"In here," Asher called.

I found him in the tearoom, sitting in front of the puzzle I'd put out that morning. He stared at the pieces with such concentration, I almost wondered if he might lift one with his energy. I knew from experience, the bursts of energy he could emit were usually emotionally driven, intense, and very difficult to control.

"Hey …" The greeting tiptoed out of me as I read the tightness of Asher's features and thought about how he must've been worried about me. I was supposed to meet him downtown, and I'd bailed to go investigate Meadow. "I'm so sorry. I got stuck up at The Pines …" I stopped, expecting a scolding any second.

But nothing came. He nodded, barely looked up from the puzzle.

"You okay?" I asked, walking closer.

He glanced up as if he'd just noticed me. "Sorry, I was trying to remember where these pieces are supposed to go for whenever you got back. Puzzling is definitely not a solitary activity when you don't have a body." He laughed.

"You're not mad?" I clenched my teeth into an apologetic smile.

Asher sighed. "I won't pretend that I didn't worry at first, but not having a body means I have limitations. You've shown me time and time again that you can take care of yourself, Rosemary. I need to stop being overprotective of you and let you live your life. And maybe you're right about Van. I might be judging him on the rest of his family's actions. I would hate for someone to do that to me, which means it's not fair of me to do it to him."

The speech was lovely, but that last part had me staring down at the toes of my boots.

"Well, you might not have been as far off base about Van as I thought …" I wrinkled my nose.

Asher popped up out of his chair and sped toward me. "Tell me everything." He gestured behind himself. "Library? Tea?"

"That sounds perfect."

Ten minutes later, I was changed into cozy clothes, had a blanket wrapped around my shoulders, and a hot mug of tea clutched in my hands.

"Okay, so I was downtown, trying to tell the chief about my kettle clue—"

"Trying?" Asher grimaced. "That doesn't sound good."

I got up to make a fire as I talked. "I'm nosy, and he doesn't need my help."

Asher nodded as if he already knew that and I could move on. I smiled, having missed him during my time up at The Pines.

"But I did learn that Cinder has an airtight alibi which turned out to be a video of him eating a hamburger at a fast-food joint out of town during the time Clover was killed." I stopped for effect, my eyes widening in the same way the woman's had when she'd told me. And in the same way she'd realized I didn't get why that was a big deal, I noticed Asher's lack of reaction. "He's internet famous for being a hardcore vegan," I said.

Asher's face lit up in recognition now. "Ah, so that's why he lied about being with Meadow the whole time. He didn't want to ruin his career."

"Exactly. Which was why Meadow was so upset that she'd ruined things for him. Her time line didn't match up with his because he left her yurt. I'm guessing he went to go have the fight with Clover one person witnessed. Then Jolene and I encountered him in a full rage right after. He must've been walking to his car to go get the burger, not to kill Clover."

Asher sat back. "Okay, then. So now Meadow doesn't have an alibi for the time of the murder. And she was the one to find Clover's body. Is there any reason she would kill her friend?"

This was why I loved talking with Asher. We thought so similarly. "Well, it just so happens that I found these." The fire looked like it was catching, so I held up a finger and ran to grab the pictures from my jacket pocket in the entryway. Fingers lingering on Abigail's journal, I left it in the pocket … for now. Maybe I would take a peek inside to make sure there wasn't anything potentially hurtful before sharing it with Asher.

Returning with the Polaroids, I splayed them on the coffee table in between us. The word LIAR scrawled across Clover's face looked even more menacing seeing it for the second time. And Van's lie about not knowing Clover seemed even worse seeing his lips pressed against hers again. A gust of wind shoved a tree limb up against the window, making me jump.

Shaking off the momentary scare, I said, "But while I was there snooping around and finding these, the second wave of the storm hit, and I got pulled inside with Van and the rest of the community members."

Asher's eyebrows rose with interest. "That must've been fun." He rolled his eyes.

If he'd grown up in the nineties like I had, he would've definitely added the word NOT to the end of that statement.

"Yeah, not so much. But it was informative. I met SJ's ghost." I watched Asher take in this information.

The empathy he'd been working on feeling for Van must've really gone a long way because he didn't tense up or scowl like he had been whenever I'd mentioned any of the Sullivans. Instead, he merely looked interested. "Informative meaning you learned whether or not the rumor about him stealing your great-grandfather's company was true?"

I shook my head. "It's not true. There were financial records for his company dating back decades that showed he took over managing the company when my great-grandfather inherited it during the Great Depression. See, Richard was a fisherman and didn't like the business side of things. SJ had been laid off from his job and wanted to help his friend. SJ saved the failing company and ran it for a decade until Richard insisted on selling it to him. He still had no interest in the company and wanted to buy a new fishing boat. From there the company grew into the one Liv now runs." I dipped my head to one side. "I think Ivan did a fair bit for the growth of the company too, but SJ had a reputation for treating his workers well and giving back to the community, unlike his son."

Asher's eyebrows arched up. "So why is SJ still here?"

I shrugged, just as SJ had done when I'd wondered the

same. "Doesn't know. He thought it had to do with making sure Ivan changed from such a Scrooge, but apparently that never happened, and now Ivan's dead but SJ's still here."

Asher sat there, taking it all in. I loved to hear him summarize in his own words. "So SJ and Richard were really good friends who helped each other out."

A smile crept onto my face. "The kind of friends who make each other better people," I said, quoting Van.

Asher met my gaze and matched my expression. "Ah, darn. I kinda thought our friendship was one of a kind."

I wanted to hug him. "It still is." I held up a finger. "SJ and Richard were both alive. We have something unique."

Asher chuckled. "I'll take that." A mischievous expression took over his face as if he'd forgotten he had dessert in the fridge. "Wait, so how does that make Van a suspect?"

I sat up a little straighter. "Oh, right. Well, besides Meadow's hateful additions to this photograph and others like it, take a closer look at this one." I pointed to the picture where Clover and Van were kissing in the background.

"He was in a relationship with Clover?"

"Well, they're dressed in a couple's costume so I would've thought so, but apparently they don't call them relationships anymore." Even though these people were all my age, I felt like a grandma talking about *the kids these days*. "They all seem to have these open 'things' without boundaries."

"Yeah, because that usually works well." Asher sat back after leaning forward to glance at them.

I, however, stayed leaning forward. Something about the LIAR picture caught my eye that hadn't before. "That's what I said ..." My words petered out as I peered closer.

I knew the place Meadow and Clover were at in this picture. It was a popular coffee house in downtown Portland. Unable to shake it off, I pulled my laptop from where it sat on the coffee table and opened it. I needed to check to see if I was right.

"But the even more questionable part is that he claimed he didn't know Clover before she came to the commune," I added, no longer worried about using the word Van hated.

"Obviously a lie, especially since Halloween hasn't happened yet this year, so this has to be from a previous year." Asher pointed to the Halloween picture.

"Correct. So now it seems Cinder is out as a suspect and Van and Meadow are in. If Clover was killed around seven-thirty, they both had the opportunity. Van disappeared almost immediately when we got there, and the first time I saw Meadow was when she came running to tell us about Clover."

Asher exhaled. "But letting the chief know any of this without telling him you were sneaking around in Meadow's yurt without her permission is the tricky part."

"Exactly," I said, eyes searching my computer screen as I logged into Instagram.

"What are you up to?" Asher moved next to me so he could see.

I angled the screen toward him. "I know that coffee shop." I pointed to the Polaroid. "They're all over Instagram. I just want to check." I chewed absentmindedly on my cheek as I searched.

The shop's page came up, a mixture of tiled pictures featuring artisan lattes and baked items. Scrolling down, I saw no evidence of Clover or Meadow. Trying again, I searched for the shop's hashtag instead, so I got all the posts other users uploaded from their time at the café.

About halfway down the page, I spotted the familiar, smiling faces of Clover and Meadow, both alive.

I clicked on the picture and the text loaded. "*Our personal brand is whatever the overlap between coffee and shopping is #coffeeis-life #portlandia.*" The name of the Instagram user, however, was neither Clover nor Meadow. Instead, it was posted by Courtney Sutton.

Clicking her page, I quickly realized Clover must've really been named Courtney. And I suppose it shouldn't have come as a shock. Clover and Meadow—and Cinder too—now seemed like made-up names.

"Courtney, huh?" Asher said, narrowing his eyes.

I shared his sentiment. If these women were hiding their real names, what else were they hiding?

An hour later, we'd officially gone down a few Instagram rabbit holes. We knew three things:

1. Courtney had two accounts. One was of her as a rich socialite who posted OOTDs—outfits of the day, as I learned when I looked it up—and drove a car more expensive than my house. She'd gone to a fancy prep school and an Ivy League college.

2. The other account was Clover's. That one was filled with posts about mindfulness and living "off the grid."

3. With as many Polaroids as Meadow had of her and Clover together, that picture of them in the coffee shop was the only evidence of her in Courtney's or Clover's feed. There was no mention of her name, Meadow or otherwise.

"Meadow obviously knew Clover when she was Courtney, so she knew she was lying about who she was," I mused, ruling out the possibility that Meadow had found out the truth and gotten angry with Clover for lying.

Asher pressed his lips together in concentration. "So the questions remain: Who is Meadow? What does she think Clover lied about? And did she kill her because of it?"

17

I was paying Wallace for groceries at Cove Grocer the next morning when Harriet came running inside carrying Whiskers.

Wallace and I both braced ourselves. Something happening to hurt the mayor was a constant fear of everyone in Pebble Cove. Apparently, Meow had narrowly survived a terrible bike accident about a decade earlier, an event that had been since dubbed The Great Assassination Attempt of 2010. It hadn't helped that the biker had been a visitor to town, only confirming Pebble Cove's feelings about people who didn't live here.

The current mayor was on her back in Harriet's arms, like one might hold a newborn baby. The worry I felt was clearly mirrored on Wallace's face. His curled mustache twitched like it did anytime he was uncomfortable.

"Is Whiskers hurt?" I asked while Harriet caught her breath.

The cat was pressed up against Harriet's body. But I couldn't see anything wrong with the parts of the mayor that were visible. The editor of the local paper shook her head.

"Oh. No … nothing to do with Whiskers." She glanced down at the cat who stared back at her, purring happily. "I was just holding her when I heard the news."

"What news? What's up?" Wallace asked, impatience sharpening his usually sugary-sweet tone.

"The road washed out," she said during a break between breaths, "over where Cove Drive meets up with Misty." She pointed in the general direction and looked at me. "Sorry, Rosemary. It looks like you might be stuck downtown for a while."

I wrinkled my nose, glancing outside at the fairly sunny but crisp day. "But it's not even raining anymore," I said. "How'd the road wash out?"

As if she was a geology teacher disappointed in me for asking such a question, Harriet tsked. "The amount of rain we got caused standing water in that area to loosen the ground under the road, making it unstable as it drained and eroded away earth along with the water. It doesn't need to be currently raining to fall apart."

Well, that made sense. But it was inconvenient nonetheless. It was early morning, before I'd even opened the tea shop. I'd popped into town to get a few essentials for the day and pick up my pastries from Jolene.

"It looks like I'll be spending the day at Jolene's shop, then," I said through a sigh.

Wallace nodded, and Harriet changed places with me, scratching behind Whisker's ears as she asked Wallace for a copy of today's *Portland Tribune*. The woman not only produced a weekly paper for our town but also read all the other local circulations religiously.

Toting my two bags with me, I walked down the street

toward the Pebble Cove Tea Company building. Jolene had talked about changing the name to something like Tea by the Cove to match my Tea by the Sea now that we were in business together, but we decided to give it a year to make sure everything continued to go as well as it had been for the past few months.

Remembering Tea by the Sea—and more importantly, who was there right now—I thought of Asher and how I wasn't going to be "right back" like I told him I would be. And even though he'd mentioned how he trusted me and wasn't trying to keep tabs on where I was all the time, I wished that he had some sort of ghost phone I could use to contact him. Since I didn't, I walked into Jolene's shop. At least I was somewhere he could find me this time.

"Morning," Jo called from behind the counter.

"Hey," I said, unable to keep the fatigue from my tone.

She grabbed a large to-go box. "I'll get your baked goods ready."

"Actually," I said, stopping her. "Mind if I hang out here today?"

Jolene's eyebrows shot up. She slid the box back under the register. "I'd love the company. But why? Is something wrong with your place?"

Excitement spiked through me at the realization that Jolene hadn't heard the news about the washed-out road yet. I almost laughed at myself. I was definitely becoming a Pebble Cove native if I was this excited about getting to be the first one to give her the news. Still … it was kind of a fun feeling.

"The road washed out right where Cove meets up with Misty. I can't get through until …" I shrugged, not quite sure how long it took to fix a washed-out road.

Jolene waved a hand toward me. "If they get the Rickster's road guy to do it like they did with the end of Pelican Point two years ago, it'll only take him a day. You should be back in your place by the end of the day."

I cocked an eyebrow. "The Rickster has a road guy?"

Jolene tilted her head in my direction in a "what did you expect?" gesture. "His name's even Crater Joe." She pointed to my bags. "Do you have cold stuff in there? I can stick them in the big fridge." She held out her hands.

I nodded and handed the bags over.

After Jolene stored them, we aproned up, and I turned the sign on the front door from Closed to Open. We had the most fun, and by lunchtime I was wishing I could have a coworker I didn't look crazy talking to during the day. That thought immediately made me feel awful. I wouldn't trade Asher for the world, but sometimes it felt like our friendship was a secret I wish I didn't have to keep any longer.

"Any news on that girl who was killed up at The Pines?" Jolene asked during the lull before lunch.

About to ask her why she thought I would know anything, I remembered how we'd become friends. When her ex had been poisoned at her tea shop's grand reopening, we'd worked together to find the truth about who was to blame.

"Well, that angry guy we thought did it has an alibi, so he's out. But now I'm wondering about the 'friend' who found her and Van." I rinsed out a mug before putting it in the dishwasher.

Jolene cocked an eyebrow as she reached past me to grab a dishcloth. "Van?"

I knew my friend had been hoping something would spark between Van and me. She must've thought I was pretty sad with the number of nights I stayed in and how many times she caught me chatting with myself.

"Yep," I said in response. "I think he and Clover used to date, and he lied to me about it." I went on to explain the pictures I'd found and the mysterious second identity of Clover.

"Did you tell the chief all of this?" was Jolene's first question.

I wrinkled my nose. "I didn't exactly come upon those photographs in a way he or the law would approve of."

"I see." She tapped her fingernails on the countertop. "So how could you let him know without letting him know how you know?"

We laughed at the complicated sentence. Truthfully, the situation felt equally as complicated.

"Emails and phone calls are all traceable. And as much as I'd like to help, I also really don't want to get in trouble or give the chief another reason to hate me. I thought about a handwritten note left at the station, or maybe a carrier pigeon. Are we sure the owl thing from Harry Potter was definitely all magic or could we try something like that?" I chewed on my lip as I thought.

Jolene chuckled.

"Or maybe it doesn't even matter," I offered. "The last time I tried to tell him something helpful, he already had the information and made it very clear he didn't need me to butt in." Plus, I realized, the photograph of Van and Clover kissing was Meadow's, so maybe she'd already told the police that Van knew Clover and my clue was redundant, yet again.

Jolene pressed her lips forward. "True. I mean, there's really no obligation on your part to get involved. In fact, considering how the last case turned out for us, maybe it's better if you stay out of it."

The previous time I'd looked into a murder case, Jolene

and I had ended up held at gunpoint by three separate Panamanian arms dealers. We both shivered at the memory.

Glancing at the clock, Jolene said, "If you need a break, now is a great time. Not that I don't usually do this by myself anyway, but the next half hour is pretty dead. I'm guessing it'll be even slower because no one from the spit can make their way into town until that road is fixed."

"Actually," I said, glancing over at my jacket hanging in the hallway to the back room. "I do need to pop over to the library. Do you mind?"

Jolene snorted. "If I did, I'd be out of luck every day. You know what it's like."

Of course I did. Working alone was our normal. A couple of hours with a coworker and I'd forgotten.

"I'll be back in a few," I said as I pulled on my jacket, eyeing the sky through Jolene's large picture windows facing the cove. Clouds hung overhead but they were generally light and fluffy, nothing like the gray monsters from the past few days. Still, I wasn't about to take any chances.

Also, I needed the jacket so I could bring Abigail's journal with me without drawing too much attention to it. While there were a few buildings too new for Asher to step foot inside, the library was the one that made the most sense to have a book. So it was a place where I could check out the contents safely before sharing them with Asher. SJ's hesitation to read through them had made me wary.

I wasn't ten feet from the door of the tea shop when Asher appeared next to me on the boardwalk.

"Hey," he said with a smile. "Sorry you got caught on this side."

A few people outside for a lunchtime walk passed by at that moment, so I couldn't respond right away. Seeing even more people walking up ahead, I remembered my trick from the other day. Sure, it had *almost* backfired in front of the chief, but it was worth a try.

Taking out my phone, I held it to my ear. Shooting Asher a grin, I said, "Hello. Yes, crazy, huh? Jolene and I have been having fun working together, so it's okay."

Asher's blue eyes almost twinkled. "Great idea. And what a nice change for the two of you." He nodded. "I'm sure it gets lonely being the only one every day."

Asher didn't say this with any sense of sarcasm or ill feelings. He genuinely seemed to understand that not having someone else to talk to throughout the day must be difficult.

"Yeah, but poor Jolene doesn't have someone to make faces at when the Rickster uses his finger to stir his tea, or to laugh with when Daphne inevitably gets the pieces of a sugar packet stuck in her oversprayed hair," I said.

Asher chuckled, looking toward the library where we'd continued to walk as we talked. "You checking out a book?" he asked.

A family passed by us, but it wasn't their presence that made my face turn hot, then cold. I should've been able to answer, no problem with my new talking-on-the-phone disguise. But what bothered me was the fact that I was going to the library because Asher couldn't step one ghostly foot inside. My fingers ran along the edge of Abigail's diary in my pocket.

I was, yet again, hiding things from him.

He was working on trusting me, trying not to worry I might get killed everywhere I went without him. I thought back to the way that had made me feel last night. The answer, above all else, was it made me feel respected. And here I was doing the exact opposite to him.

Asher was strong. He'd handled it when we thought he

was a World War I deserter, and he could handle whatever Abigail had written in this diary. This was his story after all.

I stopped, keeping my phone pressed to my ear even though I looked him straight in the eyes. "Ash, I'm so sorry. I was actually going in there to read … this." I pulled the diary out of my pocket, realizing at the last second that it didn't have any writing on the outside so he wouldn't know what it was. "SJ pointed it out to me when I was stuck in the library up at The Pines during the storm yesterday. It's Abigail's diary."

Asher's expression had frozen in concern when I'd turned to him, but at these words, it fell flat. "Oh. W-wow." He shook his head. "Uh—I don't know what to say."

"I didn't tell you about it because I wanted to see what it said before I shared it with you." I cringed as I watched him take in that admission.

But I didn't expect the smile that he gave me in return. "To try to protect me from things that are out of your control. We are well suited to be friends, aren't we?" He laughed, the motion making his eyes squint and crinkle at the edges.

I couldn't help but follow suit. "Yeah, we are. And I know now that last night when I realized you weren't worried about me, it took a weight off my shoulders."

Asher nodded emphatically. "I can't tell you how much it hurt thinking of you having to keep that awful knowledge about me possibly deserting to yourself for so long before we found out the truth." He narrowed his eyes as he focused in on me. "No more secrets, Rosie. We've got to trust one another."

"Deal. Yes. Absolutely."

I wanted to reach out and fake shake his ghostly hand,

but there really were a lot of people around, and that would, for sure, look crazy.

Motioning to the bench behind us, I said, "Want to look through it with me?"

Asher held his hand out. "After you."

I sat down, propping my phone against my ear with my shoulder so I could use both hands to hold open the journal. The position was awkward though, so I grabbed my earbuds from my pocket and plugged them into my phone. I hoped setting it on the bench next to me would keep up the illusion I was talking on the phone.

Asher settled next to me as I was putting in my earbuds. Even though only one of us could technically breathe, we both inhaled before I opened to the first page.

18

The first entry in Abigail's diary was from the fall of 1911. As I scanned through the handwritten page, words and phrases jumped out at me: *Moving, Pebble Cove, nervous … Asher.*

We seemed to reach the line about *the most handsome boy I've ever laid eyes on* at the same time. Asher grinned like the high school boy he was when they'd met.

Clearing his throat, he said, "To be fair, she moved from one small town to another."

"Aww. Don't sell yourself short, my friend. When I first met you, I thought you were quite handsome."

"But now that you know me, that's all changed?" He snorted.

"You know what I mean." I leaned to one side. If Asher had a body, I would've knocked my shoulder into his playfully. As it was, my shoulder hit no resistance, and I almost fell over onto the bench. I righted myself, and readjusted my earbuds.

"Next page, then?" I asked, flipping forward to cover my embarrassment.

After that, it was Asher's turn to look embarrassed. The next few pages were chock full of Abigail in full teenage-crush mode. She waxed poetic about Asher's eyes and then his lips and then his hair and even his feet.

I stopped to glance down at his feet. They were covered in a smart pair of brown leather oxfords like always.

"What are you doing hiding your 'gorgeous toes' away in those shoes all the time?" I joked through a giggle, quoting her exact words from the page.

Asher's face wrinkled into an embarrassed frown. "They're regular feet."

"I don't believe you. I need to see them. Can you take those off?" I asked.

He shrugged. "I don't think I can." He brought a foot and pulled on the shoe, but it wouldn't come off. "I showed up wearing this when I became a spirit. It's obviously not what I was wearing when I died."

He'd been buried with his army tags, which meant he'd probably been in uniform when he was killed, especially given he was likely on his way to meet up with his unit before deployment.

"Maybe I manifested in an outfit that fit my personality the most." He shrugged.

Turning to face him, I forgot about the book in my lap for a moment. "But wait. You can manipulate your hair and your suspender straps, so why can't you take off your shoes?" True to form, the moment I felt like I might be getting a hang of this whole seeing-ghosts thing, something new and inexplicable came to smack me in the face.

"You're right." Asher ran his thumbs up and down the inside of the suspenders as if to prove my point.

When he exhaled and shook his head a moment later, I pointed at him. "That's it!"

A couple walking past at that exact moment stopped and peered in the direction I was pointing, unable to see Asher sitting next to me. Thankfully, I still had my phone sitting next to me, obviously hooked up to the earbuds. I could see through Asher in his translucent away-from-home state and knew Jolene's shop was in line with where I was pointing.

"That's the best tea in town," I added with a smile.

The couple moved on, but I heard the wife ask her husband, "Doesn't she own that place?" before they walked away.

Asher took a few seconds to stop laughing before I could explain what my eureka moment had been before that interruption. Even then, I had to restart three times because he broke out into another set of guffaws at the memory of the couple's faces.

"Okay, what's it?" he asked, swiping at his eyes.

"That," I said, refraining from pointing again. "You swiped at your eyes, but you don't have tears … or eyes, really. You inhale and exhale even though you don't need to breathe. You blink, run your hands through your hair, and mess with your suspenders because all of these things were habits you've carried over from when you were alive."

Asher nodded along as I talked. "That does make sense."

We sat there for a moment while I basked in my discovery before I remembered what we were doing. "Oh, right. Let's get back to your amazing feet." I tittered.

Asher made a circle with his hand in front of me. "We can skip ahead. Try to find where she meets Sully. That's what we're trying to figure out: if Abigail knew of Sully's plan to kill me, or even better, how he did it."

I swallowed any protestations about how we weren't sure

Sully was the killer—it wasn't the time to argue—and turned a few pages forward, scanning for Sully's name.

Before I could spot anything of the sort, my attention caught on something else. Right in front of Jolene's shop, a black Tesla pulled into one of the slanted parking spaces along the boardwalk.

Noticing my focus had shifted, Asher followed my gaze. "Who's that?"

"I don't know, but they almost ran me over last night when I was leaving The Pines. Meadow was in the back seat with them."

Out of the car emerged a middle aged man and woman, both wearing impeccable designer clothes. They disappeared into the tea shop.

Asher looked at me and then down at the diary in my hands. "We can finish this later. Let's go see who those two are."

I didn't need to be told twice. Shoving the diary back into one pocket and my phone into another, I headed toward the tea shop. Jolene was taking their orders as I entered. Realizing I still wore the earbuds, I plucked them from my ears and added them to the pocket holding my phone.

"Did you want the same thing you had yesterday or something new?" Jolene asked, sending a quick glance in my direction as I hung up my jacket and put my apron back on.

Jolene might've been wondering why I'd only been gone about ten minutes, instead of taking longer for my break, but if she was, she didn't say anything about it.

"Can we do a pot of the Home blend?" the woman asked. "We're missing ours today and could use some comfort."

Jolene tipped her head to one side. "Of course you can. Any word on when you'll get to go back?"

"As of now, we're still waiting for the chief to release her body. He says it might be a bit before he can get the investigation wrapped up." Her shoulders sagged.

The man next to her sniffed back a tear and raised his hand to cover his face.

My heart ached. These must be Clover's parents … sorry, Courtney's.

"Where are the two of you staying, then?" Jolene asked, realizing they couldn't have come from The Pines if the road was washed out.

"Oh, at the Gull's Nest." The woman pointed behind her toward the fire station.

Pebble Cove wasn't known as a tourist destination, so we didn't have any hotels, but there was a bed-and-breakfast for the occasional family member who came into town or tourists who stumbled upon the place without realizing there wasn't anything particularly touristy to do here.

"Good," Jolene said, settling her elbows on the counter. "I'm sure Georgie's taking good care of you then."

They nodded and said she was.

"I'll start that tea order," I said to Jolene, getting to work behind her.

They sent sad smiles in my direction. I couldn't bear to hold their eye contact too long before I turned back to the tea making to keep myself from joining them in their tears.

I'd never met Courtney. And even though I'd attended her memorial service and heard countless stories about her through the community members, there was something so intimate about meeting the people who brought her into this world.

Asher floated around with me behind the counter, trying

to avoid Jolene so he wouldn't give her any unnecessary chills.

"They were the ones who brought Meadow back to The Pines yesterday, the ones who almost ran you over?" he asked.

Unable to speak an answer, I glanced over at Jolene to make sure she was busy before nodding in response.

"And so they were the ones Meadow was meeting with yesterday as well," Asher said, not really seeming to expect an answer but just as if he were thinking out loud.

I set the teapot steeping on the counter while I wrestled with my thoughts. On one hand, Courtney's parents might be able to give me good information about Meadow and how she knew their daughter. On the other, it felt completely crass to ask anything of the grieving parents. As if my thoughts were a Ping-Pong ball bouncing from one side of the net deciding what was moral, I recognized one of the greatest things I could give them right now was closure. If the killer was caught and the case closed, they could take their daughter's remains home.

Asher watched me as if he knew the mental struggle I was going through. He sent me an encouraging smile as I took the teapot and some cups over to their table a few minutes later when the leaves were properly steeped.

The couple looked up at me expectantly when I arrived at their table. I thought I saw a flicker of recognition flash over their faces at the sight of me, confirming they'd seen me running down the hill away from The Pines.

I set the kettle in between them and then a teacup and saucer in front of each person. I opened my mouth, questions about Meadow at the ready. Behind those sat a line of questions about Courtney and her Clover personality. Did they know their daughter was posing as a different person? Had that been the thing that had gotten her killed?

My stomach flipped uncomfortably. In that moment, I knew I couldn't do this. As much as my motivation was to help, I saw how it could be misconstrued as small-town gossip and nosiness. I needed to let the chief handle this one.

I turned my face into the most warm, supportive version of itself and said, "Let me know if I can get you anything else" instead.

They thanked me, but before I turned to leave, I froze. There was *one* question I needed to ask.

"What about something from our bakery case?" I checked with Jolene, who stood behind the counter. She gave me a nod, sharing the same thought. "On the house, of course."

The couple said they'd love to try Jolene's cinnamon cake. Jo heard them and got to work plating a couple slices. Asher clapped a few times to show his approval as I rejoined him behind the counter.

I let Jolene take it to their table. She'd made it, after all, and this way I wouldn't be tempted to ask anything of them again. The way the couple picked at the pieces of cake instead of devouring them like I usually did told me I'd made the right decision in letting them mourn in peace.

"Thank you so much. This town has been so supportive and sweet. It really means the world to us right now," the woman said, catching Jolene before she walked away.

Jolene nodded. "Anything we can do. We're so sorry for your loss."

The woman's face looked like it was about to fracture, but she took a deep breath and kept her composure. "We're just glad she was in such a wonderful place with a good friend by her side."

My ears perked up from where I stood behind the counter. A good friend. Meadow. They didn't know the truth about her strained relationship with their daughter or why she thought Courtney was a LIAR. I didn't need to ask any questions of them to know that was another mystery to add to the pile.

But right when I thought I'd figured that out, Courtney's father said, "Yeah, well by her side or not, Van couldn't protect her this time."

Asher met my eyes with his. So the good friend wasn't Meadow, but Van instead. Suddenly his lie about having just met Clover when she moved to the community seemed a lot more sinister.

19

Wringing my hands in anticipation, I made myself walk forward. "I'm going to tell him the truth, and then I'll be done with this case," I reiterated to Asher as he followed me down Cove Drive and toward the police station.

I adjusted the phone I'd pressed against my ear to look at him. Doubt made uncomfortable ridges form on his forehead, but he nodded all the same.

"Okay, be calm and … maybe don't show him the pictures unless you have to," he said. "See if he'll listen to what you have to say first."

"Right. The chief listening to me." I snorted. "I'll eat my jacket if that happens."

Asher gave me a salute as he stayed behind on the sidewalk, and I continued forward to the station door. I passed by Officer Kennedy as I approached, realizing I still had my phone to my ear.

"Okay, Mom. Talk to you soon. Love you," I said to no one, smiling like a normal person on the phone with her mother.

It seemed to work because Kennedy smiled back.

One last inhale for strength, and I was walking inside the station.

Police Chief Clemenson pressed his lips together and watched me. His silence was unnerving, so I filled it by babbling more than I had during the previous five minutes.

"I'm sure you're already looking into Meadow, but I wanted to let you know about the pictures I saw when I was in her yurt the other day."

"Right." The chief eyed me. "So Meadow just happened to have a bunch of these pictures where she'd written LIAR across the victim's face lying around, for anyone to see?"

Clearing my throat, I said, "Well, I have really good eyesight, so maybe she didn't realize I could see them." I could feel my cheeks heating up with anxious energy. "And then there was the fact that Van told me he didn't know Clover before she came to the commune, and yet her parents told me they were old friends." I thanked her parents for that so I didn't have to bring up the pictures again.

The chief sighed, his large chest heaving out in the process. "Is that all, Miss Woodmere?"

I stood. "Yes, thanks for listening. I know you're doing your job. This isn't a commentary on that. I'm not doing this because I think you're not investigating. I wanted to make sure you knew what I knew." I cleared my throat. "And you probably did, but I wouldn't have been able to forgive myself if you didn't and I hadn't said anything, you know?"

The chief's face softened. "Thank you, Rosemary."

And even though the man didn't seem happy, he didn't seem angry with me either. I was going to count that as a win.

I scrambled out of there before I did something to ruin the victory.

"Good?" Asher said when I met up with him outside the station.

I nodded, then turned the motion into a head tip. "Definitely not bad. I might actually have to eat my jacket."

"Please don't." Asher chuckled. "I'll happily let you out of that promise."

We walked back toward Jolene's tea shop. It had been slow before I'd left for the station, but I told her I would come back and keep her company for the last hour of the day. The moment I opened the tea shop door, however, Jolene waved me away.

"The road's open. You're free!" She grinned. "Thanks for your help today."

"My pleasure. We really should consider working together more often."

She agreed and we said our goodbyes as I grabbed my groceries from her fridge.

Asher and I made our way back to Tea by the Sea—him via split-second ghostly travel and me via the new road.

The Rickster's road guy was packing up his supplies. I mean, I assumed the only man left was Crater Joe. The rest of his team of workers pulled away while he cleaned up the last bit of machinery. It seemed like a boss thing to do. Plus, he looked like someone named Crater Joe. Between his scraggly gray hair, sad eyes, long nose, and furrowed expression, the man could've been a cross between a human and a mountain troll.

He gave me a salute as I drove over the black, newly laid

roadway. A little nervous about possibly being the first one to drive on this new section, I rolled down my window and waved to him.

"Thank you!"

At this, his sad face brightened and he waved back. "My pleasure." Seeing the way I was crawling over the new section, he added, "No need to be gentle. That road's as sturdy as a new pair of underwear now."

A little uneasy about his choice of comparison, I rolled up my window. I drove the rest of the way at a normal speed and wondered what kind of underwear Crater Joe must have in his closet.

Back at the house, I checked the weather forecast quickly, making sure there weren't any more storms on the horizon before I turned on the gas and furnace again. The heat it pumped into the house made everything feel better.

"Do you want to keep reading through Abigail's diary?" I asked Asher as we settled into the library. It was only an hour before our usual closing time, so I'd just kept the Closed sign on the front door.

Asher's eyes sparkled. "I thought you'd never ask."

Grabbing the journal from my coat pocket, I flipped to the general place we were at before. Asher joined me on the couch so he could read along with me.

"Okay, so we're searching for anything about Sully …" I said as I let my attention flit over the page.

Asher grumbled something unintelligible, but I could see him scanning too.

And two pages later, we found it:

> I ran into Sullivan Mills today at the mercantile. As poorly as Asher always spoke of him, I expected the man to be a complete oaf. But actually, he was quite

> sweet. We had a good talk while we walked by the water.

From reading the previous entries, I knew this was a few months into Asher's time away at college.

"And so it began," Asher said.

As much as he blew it off, said he was over it, and pretended not to care that she'd found someone else, I could see it still bothered him. I flipped further, looking for Sully's name. It appeared more as the entries progressed through time. It was a sad inverse relationship: the more she wrote about Sully, the less there was about Asher. Soon Abigail's written thoughts turned to guilt and how she wished she hadn't promised her hand to Asher.

It was clear from her writing that Sully had convinced her that Asher had used his intellectual way of speaking to lure her into an engagement.

> I was adamant with Sully that it wasn't like that. Asher and I did have a connection when I first moved to town. Though even as I professed the legitimacy of our relationship, I doubted it too. I think I might … I think I *have* fallen for Sully.

It was uncomfortable, to say the least.

"Ash, we can take a break from reading. This can't be easy." I closed the diary until it was only open a crack.

Asher's face was tight, but he gestured toward the diary. "No, it's okay. We only have a little left. I can handle it."

He was right. We were nearing the end of the pages. A quick glance at the clock on the wall confirmed that it was closing in on four in the afternoon. The next section was clearly the infatuation stage, only this time the object of her affection was Sully. Just as she'd done with Asher, she marveled at Sully's good qualities, though I noticed she didn't write quite as much about how handsome or kind Sully was, and definitely nothing about his gorgeous toes.

For obvious reasons, we read through that section quickly, neither of us wanting to linger in those descriptions. The next set of entries proved to be equally as difficult to get through, but for a completely different reason. Abigail detailed the time when Asher came home after graduation, and when she told him she was no longer in love with him.

> I could see it in his eyes. He knew. He'd known for a while now. Whatever Sully might say about the man, when he offered to let me out of our engagement, I knew he was a good soul. In that moment, I have to admit I was a bit sad, and I wondered if I'd made the right decision. Though I suppose it didn't matter in the least, because when we went to tell Daddy, he forbade us from calling off the wedding. He wouldn't say as much in front of Asher, but I know it's due to the money the Bensons have, and the lack of money the Mills possess.

Even though it all happened a century ago, reading Abigail's thoughts about it made it feel like we were in the midst of the drama. Seeing we only had one page left, I flipped it over to see if there was anything on the back.

One final sentence occupied the last page. And whereas most of Abigail's writing had been in past tense, reflecting on the things that had already happened that day, the last sentence was in present, looking forward to the future.

> Diary, I'm honestly so scared about what Sully will do when I tell him I'm still going to marry Asher.

20

Asher and I glanced up from Abigail's diary and met each other's equally wide eyes.

"See?" Asher said at the same time that I said, "That's all?"

After this page was the back leather cover of the diary. That was it.

"There's proof right there Sully had to be the one to kill me." Asher moved like he was going to jab at the book, but his ghostly finger simply went through the thing.

Holding my hands up, I let the diary fall into my lap. "At the risk of sounding like the chief here, we can't come to a conclusion based on a hunch."

Asher began to pace. He didn't say anything, but I could tell his thoughts were spiraling into a direction that might very well be wrong.

Deciding it might be best to distract him, I said, "SJ said his mother was a writer her whole life; she wrote things down to process them." I waved the book toward him. "This can't be her only diary. There has to be more." I grabbed my keys from the table. "I'm going to go back to The Pines and find the rest of her diaries."

Still catching up, it seemed, Asher's mouth opened then closed. "Okay," he said after a moment. "Is there anything I can do?"

"You could come with." I suggested over one shoulder. "I know you won't be able to come inside with me, but you could hang out at the edge of the property and keep and eye on the situation."

Asher nodded, looking excited for the first time at the mention of a trip to The Pines. I'd greatly underestimated him, I realized. By trying to protect him from information or situations that might be difficult, I hadn't given him a chance to show me that he was strong and could handle it. Just as I'd done with myself when I'd shut myself away and stopped trying new things, meeting new people, or putting myself out there because I'd gone through trauma in my life.

Boy, had I been wrong to worry, in both our cases.

Here he was able to read through a whole diary documenting how the woman he once loved had fallen out of love with him and in love with his mortal enemy. And now he was willing to go to the place he'd been killed, to help me.

We were made of stronger stuff, he and I—even though I wasn't 100 percent sure what Asher was made of … light particles?

The drive up to The Pines was quick, though not quite as much as the trip I'd made yesterday when I'd been on my way to search through Meadow's yurt. Also, unlike last time, I parked in the lot by the house instead of down the hill.

Outside my car, I reveled in the cool air and beautiful cacophony of birdsong coming from the forest. If I didn't know the evil things that had taken place on this property, it might've fooled me.

A quick peek into the community field, and I found Asher waiting at the edge of the woods. He waved at me and then pointed exaggeratedly toward the garden in the middle of the yurts. Van was there, working with a few other community members.

I gave Asher a smaller wave—not wanting to bring any more attention to myself than necessary. The house was unlocked and community members were allowed to come and go, so I wasn't technically breaking in, but I also didn't want to have to explain to Van why I was searching through his library. I sent one last glance toward Asher before jogging up the front steps to the farmhouse.

Inside the house was quiet in that not-very-quiet way old houses like mine had. There were a few loud clocks ticking, the wood creaked and groaned as I shut the door, and the history of it all seemed like there was a person inside with me, hanging over my shoulder.

Going straight down the hall, I entered the library.

"SJ," I whispered, "are you here?"

I glanced around when I didn't see him and figured I could search by myself if I needed to. Locating the place on the shelf where a spot still sat open for the first diary, I scanned the surrounding area. There weren't any other diaries that matched this one. I slid it back into place. I was about to pull another promising journal out when footsteps rang out behind me.

Definitely not SJ, then.

"Rosemary?"

I wheeled around and stood face-to-face with Van. Darn.

He held his gardening gloves and swiped at his forehead with the back of one hand.

"What are you doing here?" he asked. There was something behind his eyes. I couldn't tell if it was merely confusion or if there was something more sinister in his expression.

"I—uh …" I pointed in a few directions before saying, "They didn't tell you I was here?"

He raised an eyebrow. "They?"

I snapped my fingers. "Um, that guy with the hair ..." I made an indistinct motion toward my head. "I can't remember his name, but he said he would tell you I was waiting for you in the library."

Van wrinkled his nose. But before he could say anything more, Liv raced inside. In contrast with the first time we'd met, Van's sister was nothing like her cool, collected self. Her face was red and eyes narrowed. Her rigid posture told me something wasn't right.

"Van, why did I get a call from the insurance company's fraud department investigating you for saying you lost a ten-thousand-dollar engagement ring?" She put her hands on her hips. Her face softened as she noticed me behind the chair. "Oh, sorry. I didn't know you were here …"

"Rosemary," I filled in the blank for her.

"Let's talk in the hall," Van said, placing a hand on his sister's arm and leading her out of the room.

Unfortunately, the old house was echoey and did nothing to dampen the sound, especially not when Liv said, "Tell me it wasn't for her. After all that she—and you …" Liv's high heels clicked as she paced in the hallway.

Feeling awkward and wrong standing there eavesdropping, I kept looking for the next of Abigail's diaries to busy myself.

I could still hear Van as he said, "She was going to say yes. I know it. She would've …" His eagerness ebbed, and the last part of the statement sounded more like a plea than an assurance.

"So the ring is still on her?" Liv spat out the question.

But before she could say anything more, there was a knock at the front door.

"Van, this isn't good." Liv's tone dropped into a low warning. "This really isn't good."

There was a hesitation in both of their footsteps before they walked down the hall to answer the door. I ran over to the bay window that would give me a glimpse of the parking lot. Chief Clemenson's SUV was parked next to my car. The front door creaked open, but it was too far for me to hear anything. Pressing myself against the window, I watched as the chief led Van to his vehicle, and Liv got in her blue Porsche and followed.

I needed to tell Asher to get downtown and get Lois inside that station so she could find out what they had on Van. My thoughts replayed their conversation. *A ten-thousand-dollar engagement ring.*

Van's question about, *Should I say it was stolen?* stood out in my memory. The question he'd crossed out. So his phone call the other day must've been to the insurance agency about the engagement ring. Next, my thoughts went further back, to the night of the full moon gathering. Kennedy had found something in Clover's hand, something he'd called the chief over to see.

I was pretty sure Van's engagement ring was sitting in the evidence locker down at the station.

So Van really had known Clover—well, Courtney. Between the ring, her parents' mention of the history between Van and Courtney, and Van's lies about both, it was pretty clear the chief had taken the right man down to the station.

Maybe I didn't need to have Lois listen in on the interrogation after all. Of course, that thought could've been brought on by laziness, because I really didn't want to run all the way to the edge of the property to tell Asher. I chose to believe it was because I really trusted that the police had this wrapped up.

Then why did I have a bad feeling about it? There was a prickly sensation on the back of my neck.

"A pity. He was a good boy. But maybe he had more of his father in him than I thought."

I jumped, slamming my forehead into the glass. When I turned around, SJ stood behind me, leaning forward to watch the scene.

Rubbing at my forehead, I said, "Ouch. You snuck up on me."

He cocked a gray eyebrow. "Snuck up on a sneaker."

I wrinkled my nose. The ghost had a point. I had entered the house uninvited.

"I'm not trying to sneak. I was looking for you."

"Ah, and what can I do for you?" he asked, moving like he might settle into one of the armchairs.

I wanted to join him, to sit and chat about his mother and father and anything he might be able to tell me about Asher's past. But the tightness in my chest and prickly heat on my neck wouldn't go away. There was something wrong with this situation.

Because what SJ had said didn't match up. Van wasn't his father's son. He didn't solve things with anger or violence. He was kind, and no matter what the facts looked like right now, I couldn't accept he'd done this without learning a little more.

"Before we talk about that, can you do me a favor?" I said.

He nodded, waiting for my ask.

"There's a ghost waiting for me at the edge of the property down by where they discovered that body a few months earlier. Can you tell him we need eyes in the station stat? Tell him I'll be down there as soon as I can." I thought through the message and felt good about what I was asking.

"Back in a second." SJ saluted me and then disappeared.

I sat in one of the chairs to wait. And while it was more than a second, SJ returned a minute or so later.

"Nice fellow, that Asher. A pity my dad killed him." SJ took a seat in the chair across from me.

If I'd been drinking anything, I would've shot it out of my nose and sprayed it halfway across the room. As it was, I choked on my spit and dry-coughed out a strangled, "What?"

SJ hooked a thumb back toward the trees. "Your friend, Asher. He told me he thinks my dad killed him. I couldn't argue with the man."

Apparently, Asher shared none of my reservations about accusing this man's father of murder.

"Do you have any actual evidence?" I narrowed my eyes.

"Nope, but sounds like something my father would do. I know he hated those Bensons more than anything. I never heard the end of it. And given Asher's history with my mother …" SJ shrugged.

"Not to mention the line we read in her diary last night," I mumbled, more to myself than to the ghost in the room, but when he looked at me in question, I repeated it for him. "She said she was scared of what your father would do when she told him she was still going to marry Asher."

SJ whistled. "Yeah, the man had a temper at the best of times."

"That's actually what I came to ask you." I pointed to the shelf, where I'd replaced Abigail's diary. "I brought back the diary but wanted to ask if you'd ever come across any others. It ended so abruptly and so early on in her life, I feel like it can't be the only one. Are you sure there aren't more somewhere?"

"Not that I know of." He shook his head.

"There was another diary over there." I glanced toward the gold gilt lettering professing as much, the one I'd thought was Abigail's, yesterday, when I'd been searching.

"That's mine, actually." SJ chuckled. "Your great-grandfather gave that to me, actually. A joke, but one that I ended up utilizing. He made fun of me for my poetry, but I knew he was proud of me. I think buying me that diary was his roundabout way of supporting me."

As much as I loved hearing about Richard and SJ's friendship, I had to get back to Abigail's diary. I mean, it was possible the others had been lost, but her having only one, and for it to stop at such a crucial time in her life, didn't make sense.

"There are her letters, however," SJ said when he saw the look of disappointment on my face. "I think there's a box of them somewhere." He furrowed his forehead for a moment before getting up from the chair and floating around the room. "Yes, here." SJ hovered next to a smaller bookshelf on the other side of the room. Tucked into the corner was a hatbox. He pointed straight at it. "I found it hidden under the floorboards of my mother's bedroom when she died and I was demolishing the old house to build this one."

The fact that she'd hidden the letters made excitement

prick at my skin like goosebumps. "You don't mind if I borrow them?" I asked, gesturing toward the box. "I'll bring them back, like I did with the diary. I promise. You have no idea what your help means to me. To us."

SJ snorted. "I would give you a signed confession to murder if I could."

I gave him a sidelong glance. "That's not a real thing, is it?"

"I'm afraid not." SJ laughed. "In fact, I've been racking my brain for anything my father may have said. It was, of course, before I was born. But if I think of anything, I'll let you know. You live in the Benson house now?"

"Yes, and thank you." I slid the box from the shelf, sneezing as a plume of dust wafted off it. "And I'm sorry for not being candid before. I didn't know how you'd take it, me accusing your father of murder and all."

"My dear ..." The kindest smile I think I've ever seen wrinkled SJ's face. He looked at me like I was his own child. "If my father's part in your friend's murder and my grandson's involvement in that poor woman's murder proves anything to me, it's that I didn't fit in with the Mills family. If I had a family, it was your great-grandfather and the new family we made between his wife and mine." Even though it was a wonderful thing to say, there was a sadness that ate away at the light in his eyes, like waves pulling sand out to sea.

I almost put a hand on his arm before I remembered I couldn't.

"Don't count out Van just yet." I caught SJ's gaze with mine, desperate to put some of that light back in place. "It's only a hunch, but somehow I don't believe he did this. I promise I'll find out the truth."

SJ's smile returned, and he lowered his chin as he thanked me.

I walked to my car, wondering how I'd managed to promise something else I wasn't sure I could deliver to yet another ghost.

21

Stashing the hatbox of letters in my car, I headed straight for downtown and the police station. I was hoping Asher had gotten to Lois in time and she was in there right now while the chief questioned Van.

I pulled into the parking lot by the marina when my phone rang. It was my mom.

Seeing her name reminded me how much I missed her. Before I'd moved to Pebble Cove, we saw each other almost every day. Even after I'd moved, we talked at least a few times a week. So having gone so long without chatting with her made it feel like I was missing a limb. It was also possible that my trick of lying and pretending to be on the phone with her when I was actually talking to Asher was making me feel guilty.

Knowing this was a busy time for her, I didn't want to miss the opportunity to chat, so I answered the call.

"Hey." I lengthened the word like I was greeting a long-lost friend.

"Hi." Mom did the same, and when she was done,

adding, "I've missed you. I cannot wait for this fundraiser to be over."

"I know. How are you even calling me right now?"

"Shh, don't talk too loud. They'll hear and make me go back."

We laughed together for a moment.

"Mostly I'm calling because I'm mad at you," she said finally.

"What? Why?" I asked defensively.

Mom tsked. "I had to hear from Sally that there was a young woman murdered with a teapot in your town?"

I cringed. "To be fair, Sally's the biggest gossip at the library …" My cringe deepened into a frown. "Though I'm not quite clear on how she would've heard about something that happened in our little town all the way over in Portland."

"Your little town is on the map now," Mom said matter-of-factly. "There's a whole article about it. The thing went viral within the first five hours it was posted."

"What? There's no way Harriet would do that." I shook my head even though my mother couldn't see me.

Mom knew the editor of our local newspaper almost as well as I did from our monthly book clubs. In addition to being partial to carrying around the mayor and planting kisses on Madam Mayor's little pink nose, Harriet was a shrewd and respectable reporter. She only ran stories she'd triple fact checked herself and had edited to remove any bias—even the article she ran announcing Whiskers as the new mayor earlier this year contained the line, *"Some say Whisker's pink nose is the cutest thing they've ever seen. Others may feel differently, of course. As for this writer, I'm leaning toward the former."*

Any article Harriet ran on the murder would be factual

and respectful. Sadly, those two things did not usually make for viral material.

"It wasn't Harriet. It's some young blogger. Said she was undercover at the commune where the murder happened. She wrote a whole long piece about it, and it's chock full of scandal."

"Undercover?" I asked in a whisper as I thought through the faces of the community members. "What was her name?"

"Penny Meadows," Mom said after a moment as if she had to scroll to the bottom of the article to find it.

Breath caught in my throat. "Meadow?" Instantly my brain began replaying every interaction I'd had with the woman. The panic clawing at my throat reminded me she was still securely on the suspect list, with no alibi.

Maybe the assumption that the person who finds the body is the killer wasn't such a bad one after all.

"No, honey. It's Meadows, not Meadow. Penny Meadows," Mom said, breaking my concentration.

"I'm going to read it. Call you later?"

"Sure. I'll be home around seven if they unlock the chains they've tied me to my desk with." She laughed as she hung up.

My fingers trembled as I looked up Penny Meadows and Pebble Cove in the search bar of my phone's browser. The first hit was a blog titled *Girl, Thriving*. The article was called, "*Influencing the Influencer.*" I clicked on the story and read:

> Courtney was magnetic up until the moment she died. From the moment I laid eyes on her, heard her laugh, I had this need to be near her. And even though I hate her, now that she's gone, I can't deny that I sort of loved her

> too. I think we can say the same of any influencer on the scene today.

The line *until the moment she died* made me nauseous. Had Meadow been there in that moment? Had she really done this to Courtney? I read on, wondering if maybe this had gone viral because Meadow had confessed to murder via blog post.

> Maybe I just loved the me I was when I was with her. Or the way she would make me feel about myself—in the moments she wasn't putting me down or leaving me off her Instagram because I wasn't "the face people wanted."
>
> But I'm getting ahead of myself. I'll back up a little. Courtney and I met in college. We were randomly paired together in our senior creative writing class by a professor counting students off by number. And while I fell for Courtney's spark, her charisma, she fell for my words. Hard. She loved the way I wrote, complimented me like I'd never been praised before.
>
> The day she asked me to write a caption for her Instagram post, I just about died. The girl had almost a million followers. She was sure it was because she was almost as good of a writer as I was and that people found themselves in her words. I was pretty sure it had more to do with the artsy pictures she posted wearing next to nothing in her art studio living room.
>
> What I didn't know about this "great opportunity" was that my words wouldn't be attributed to me. She said not to worry about it. There was this whole plan to let everyone fall in love with my words just as she had, under the guise it was her—who they already loved—and then

she would drop the bombshell on them right before I released my first book, and I would sell a million copies.

So I did it. I jumped in with my whole heart the way an adventure junkie hurls their body out of a plane. I knew I might get hurt, but I didn't care. The endorphins I felt when I was around Courtney were all I needed. And apparently, my writing was all she needed. Her followers doubled in the first six months.

You're probably thinking I'm ridiculous right now, that I deserved what I got. And maybe I did. But so many of you who looked at Courtney and saw her life as perfect, unattainable, who judged your own lives, bodies, relationships, and experiences against hers and found that you came up short, you deserved better … deserved the truth. While I can't say I loved her writing as much as she loved mine, I will say she was a great saleswoman.

Because once we graduated and I spent more time with Courtney, I saw behind the curtain, and absolutely everything behind it was fake.

The first cracks began to show about a year ago. Her dad had gotten us what we'd both always wanted, the chance to propose a novel to an agent. He'd pulled some strings, and we needed to write a proposal, an outline, and the first three chapters for her. I wanted to write a novel; Courtney wanted to write a memoir. We ended up going with her idea. And months and months of her saying, "You do it, Pen. Write about our adventures together." I decided to write what I wanted.

And then the agent told us she needed to see a proposal by the end of the week or she was going to call it off. I ended up staying up until five in the morning writing the whole thing by myself. Courtney didn't even notice that I was writing a different outline because she was too busy hate-obsessing about trolls who kept commenting on her Instagram.

"Pen," she would say every five minutes or so, "listen to this one." And she'd read out another line about how they thought the only reason she had so many followers was because she was rich and she probably bought them. They called her a fake; they called her a liar, and every bit of it was true.

Around three in the morning, and her seven hundredth interruption, I snapped and told her she should prove them wrong. Earlier in the day, she'd been telling me all about this guy she knew from prep school—for those of you who are not millionaires, that's what the rich call high school. Anyway, this guy—who apparently I'd met at a Halloween party last year, didn't I remember?—had inherited some land in this little town on the Oregon Coast, and he was starting a peaceful living community. There would be yurts, and gardening, and probably some kind of basket weaving.

I suggested she go. She didn't have a job like I did. She should start a new Insta account under a pseudonym, and be a girl without a fancy car, or a big house, or a yacht. She could be the girl who lives in the woods and makes her own bread, and she would still get millions of followers. That was how she could prove them wrong.

Courtney danced around the living room. She made me dance with her, and then she made me promise to come with. I should quit my job. The agent was going to buy our book anyway, and we'd get a huge advance. I would be her sidekick. In return we could write about our experiences in our book. She sang the sweet promises into my ear as we pranced around my cramped living room.

After assuring me that she would unveil me as the writer behind her content at the end of the experiment, I agreed to come with.

Rain began to splatter the windshield of my car, pulling me out of the story. Seagulls cried as they circled above and dropped shelled creatures on the blacktop. I continued to read.

Being around Courtney was like having a front-row seat to adventure. She found the wildest parties and the hottest guys. While it was fun at first, watching her ditch guy after guy even though she'd just professed her undying love for them the day before, grew old. So did being the one these guys cornered to ask why she hadn't returned any of their texts.

One guy even came to her apartment in the city, singing outside her window until she ran out and danced with him in the rain. She had me take a video of them kissing, of her laughing and telling him how crazy he was but that she loved him anyway. The next day, we wrote out a caption for the video. *If love isn't half-crazy and doesn't make you kiss in the rain and sing outside windows, it's not worth it.*

Three days after that, she blocked him from her contacts. That was the side she didn't want you to see. And the next time he came around, she threatened to get a restraining order. Concerned, I'd asked her if he'd hurt her, and she told me she'd merely gotten tired of him.

Others weren't as lucky as that guy. The guy who owned the commune proposed to her within the first month we moved here even though she was seeing someone else at the same time. "I didn't say no," she told me after the proposal as she showed off the ring, "but I

> didn't say yes either." She confessed she hadn't given him a firm answer because this way we could write a couple of angsty posts about her indecision between him and the other guy before choosing neither of them.
>
> "People love a triangle," she told me when I questioned whether or not she should play with someone's heart like that. "This will get me over a million followers for sure."

I stopped reading. This didn't look good for Van. If he'd found out she was only pretending to consider his proposal to gain more social media followers, that could've very well put him over the edge.

And as much as Penny described her hate and animosity for Courtney, it didn't seem like a confession of murder. If Penny was the killer, it would seem pretty stupid to write out all the ways you hated and obsessed about your victim, and put it out there for everyone to read.

The article continued, but it was the grouping of pictures below that caught my eye. There were many of Courtney and friends, but one stood out. It was of Courtney—in what appeared to be high school, given the prep school uniform she wore—with her arm wrapped around the shoulders of Liv Mills. I read the paragraph above that I'd initially skipped over for the picture.

> She didn't care about the feelings of the boys that she hurt. And it wasn't just the guys. She treated all of her friends this way. I saw it many times and I heard all about the aftermath when those friendships imploded or, as was usually the case, exploded.

My face felt hot and cold all at once. Liv and Courtney were old friends too? They'd gone to the same prep school. I kept reading.

> Courtney told stories about the deaths of these friendships as if they were kills on a battlefield. She delighted in explaining how one friend had been too jealous of her or another was mad because her boyfriend liked Courtney better. Her favorite story was about a friend in prep school who was so bitter she hired people to slash Courtney's tires and key her car. None of the stories surprised me. Any relationship with Courtney was like the flame on a match: intense, potentially dangerous, and over quickly. I lived in constant worry about when the fire of our friendship would burn out, but I convinced myself I was different.

The story about the friend in prep school sat on my chest like a load of wet concrete. Liv's picture with Courtney was the only one that looked to be from prep school. *"She hired people to slash Courtney's tires and key her car."* What had Van said about his father? *"Hiring people to do his dirty work for him was how my father operated."*

I'd assured SJ I didn't think Van was like his father, but there was one Mills child who was.

"Liv got our father's business sense," Van had said. What if Liv was her father's daughter in more than one way? What if she shared his propensity for hiring out her dirty work?

Both she and Van had mentioned how fiercely protective of him Liv was. What if she found out about how Courtney was using her brother's engagement for social media fodder and wanted to protect him from getting hurt? It could've been the last straw in a long history of offenses between Liv and Courtney.

I glanced up at the police station. Liv was inside right now waiting for Van. How could I get in there and let the chief know he needed to question Van's sister instead? Especially when what I had wasn't much more than a hunch.

Lost in my thoughts, I almost didn't notice when a caravan of cars pulled into the parking lot. But in a town full of fishermen, where old reliable trucks and modest cars were the norm, a handful of shiny luxury vehicles definitely stood out.

I climbed out of my car, approaching the commune members as they spilled out of the cars and congregated in a circle in the parking lot.

"Hey," I said as I approached the woman who told me about Cinder the other day. "What's going on here?"

"We're here to support Van and to tell the police there's no way he could've done something to Clover."

A few people nearby chimed in with yeahs, and they began to move toward the police station.

Scanning the crowd, I asked, "Where's Meadow?"

The same woman turned to me and said, "Packing. She's going to leave as soon as the chief gives her the okay."

Eyes narrowed, I watched them flood into the police station. None of this felt right. On the sidewalk outside the station, I noticed Asher standing with Tim and Max, two of the other local ghosts.

"Hey," I said, jogging over to them, pulling my phone out and holding it to my ear in the process.

Tim and Max looked at me in confusion.

"She does that so people think she's talking on the phone instead of thinking she's crazy," Asher explained to them.

They nodded.

"Any news?" I asked.

"Apparently Meadow broke. She told them about Van and Courtney's past and how he'd proposed," Asher said.

I added this news to the tumultuous mix of information I'd just digested from the blog post. "Why didn't she tell them all of this before?" I frowned.

Asher shrugged. "She got scared after she messed up and almost got Cinder arrested, so she decided not to tell the police anything else, including the fact that Van and Courtney had known each other before or how they'd been an item since everyone moved into The Pines. Meadow was the only one who knew about them, unlike Courtney and Cinder's relationship, so no one else would've told the police."

"But when they started asking her questions that made it clear they thought she was guilty of the murder, she cracked and threw Van under the bus," Tim added.

Just as I was about to explain everything that I'd read and my wonderings about Liv, Lois came out from the station.

"My goodness." Lois shook her shoulders. "I've never been walked through so many times in my afterlife."

Asher had explained that having a living being pass through him resulted in just as eerie a feeling as it did for the person.

"It was too crowded in there. I had to get out." She rubbed her ghostly hands up and down her arms.

"Anything new?" I asked.

Lois pressed her lips together. "I don't think the kid did it. He's dumb, but not dumb enough to do something like that. Clemenson was having a heck of a time in there even before the kid's fan club showed up.

"What about Liv? Is she in the room with Van?" I asked.

Lois froze. "No, she left a bit ago. Was staring at her phone and then got really upset and darted out of there."

Panic flooded me. I glanced behind me at the parking lot. Liv's blue Porsche was gone.

22

I paced in front of the police station, my phone still glued to my ear as I talked to the ghosts.

"Did you see the direction she went?" I asked the trio of ghosts who'd been waiting outside the building.

I wanted him to say, "toward the city." I wanted to be wrong.

"Up the hill, toward The Pines. Why?" Asher asked.

He hadn't read the article I had. He didn't know Liv was a problem. The fact that she'd run to The Pines solidified my suspicions. And if she'd killed Courtney for messing with her little brother, she might be ready to do the same to Penny.

"I think Chief Clemenson has the wrong Sullivan Mills in custody," I said, my voice dry with fear. I met Asher's gaze. "Meet me up at The Pines."

And with that, I ran to my car. Asher's worried face was all I could see as I drove past and he disappeared.

Still holding my phone from when I'd been pretending to talk on it, I dialed the police station before pulling out of the lot. The call transferred to my car, and I tossed the phone onto the passenger seat, using both hands on the wheel as I pulled out onto Cove Drive and headed toward The Pines.

"Pebble Cove Police Department, this is Officer Fischer. How can I help you?" The young officer's voice cracked as he rattled off the prepared speech.

"Fischer, tell Clemenson he needs to get up to The Pines now. I think he has the wrong person. Van isn't the killer. I think it might be Liv, his sister. And I think she's going to kill Meadow-er-Penny next."

"Who is this?" Fischer asked.

"Just tell him. The Pines. Now!" I said into the speakerphone and then hung up.

I felt unsure, having no concrete reasons behind my theory, but I would rather deal with the chief coming up to The Pines and having to explain to him why I was wrong instead of not say anything and lose another life.

My car lilted a little too much on a corner, my phone shot across the seat and clattered to the floor. I didn't have time to grab it.

When I pulled up the driveway, I saw Asher standing at the edge of the woods. At the house, I screeched to a stop in The Pines' gravel lot, spraying some rocks onto Liv's car which she'd parked as haphazardly as mine.

As I exited the car, SJ was next to me.

"They're in the woods, back where your friend is. Hurry." He floated alongside me as I ran.

I'd never been so unhappy about being right, but the fear tightening SJ's features confirmed Liv wasn't up here helping Penny pack. Passing by the community garden as I ran, I grabbed a shovel just in case.

"Not sure how that's going to help you when she's got a gun, but ..." SJ shrugged.

Eyes wide, I sent a glare his way as I kept running. "A gun? Maybe lead with that before you tell me to run after them." Regardless, I kept running. Penny might be just as terrible of a person as Courtney, but neither deserved to die.

I slowed to a walk as we approached Penny's yurt. At first, I saw nothing, but then I spotted Asher standing near his gravesite.

"They're down that way," he said, not worrying about volume since SJ and I were the only ones who could hear him. "Be careful."

I followed the direction he pointed, but paused. Asher didn't move to come with. His eyes were narrowed with discomfort and worry. I realized with a spike of fear that he couldn't travel this way, never having visited this part of the forest when he was alive.

SJ could, however, and he nodded at me, sticking right by my side. I glanced back at Asher one more time before forging ahead, picking my pathway carefully along the wet forest floor.

We walked for what seemed like an hour, but was probably only a couple minutes. SJ kept sweeping forward, checking ahead, but my heart still hammered in my ears at the thought that Liv could be hiding anywhere and we could be too late to help Penny.

Bird songs echoed in the rain-soaked canopy of trees overhead. The normally delightful chirps took on an eerie tenor in the ringing silence of the forest. Once cheerful songs sounded more and more like reverberating warnings the deeper we ventured into the forest.

Just as I was about to give up, SJ put a ghostly finger to his lips and frowned.

A stick broke up ahead. A terrified cry caught in my throat, but I gulped it back down. Even among the large trunks of the coastal fir trees, I still felt exposed, dangerously unprotected. I moved behind the biggest trunk near me, my fingers digging into the damp bark as I craned my neck around.

That's when I spotted her. Liv's right arm was held up, pointing a gun at Penny, who stood next to her. Both their backs were to me.

Relief flooded me at the sight of Penny alive. Emboldened by this rush, I left the safety of my tree and scooted to the next biggest one nearer to them. Doing this once more, got me within range to hear them.

"Is it down yet?" Liv asked impatiently, glancing at the phone I now saw Penny had clutched in her hands.

"Um … almost," Penny said. "It's been shared so many times, I'm not sure what me un-publishing it will do."

"I'll worry about that part," Liv barked. "I need you to get rid of the original."

I furrowed my brow. She was having her delete the blog post.

Penny couldn't seem to help herself from testing the waters, even when she had a gun pointed at her. "Can I ask why?" she asked, glancing back at Liv. "If you hated Courtney enough to kill her, why would you care that my story reveals what a terrible person she was?"

Liv let out a snort. "I don't care about that. It's the part about my brother I need taken down. The last thing I need while I'm trying to run a company is for him to fall into depression again."

"Van was depressed?" Penny asked with a lot more sympathy than I'd be able to muster at a time like this. Maybe the girl was wasting time in hopes she'd be able to escape.

"Most people would be after being cyberbullied like he

was. And your story only makes that a possibility again. I won't see my brother go through more of that." Liv sniffed.

SJ and I looked at each other, frowned, then turned back to assess the situation.

"We could come up behind her and I could try hitting the gun out of her hand with energy," SJ said. "But her finger is clenched pretty tightly around that trigger. The burst of energy might cause the gun to go off, and it's pointed straight at the other girl."

I agreed. It seemed risky. I raised the shovel in my hands a few inches, reminding him we had at least one weapon at our disposal, but it only made his frown deepen.

"Again, if you hit her we still run the risk of the gun going off. If you can get close enough to throw the shovel the other direction, it could create enough of a distraction to get her to point the gun in a different direction so I could push it out of her hand." SJ ran his fingers along his chin as he thought.

His spirit was much dimmer here, like Asher's got when he came into town instead of staying at the house. I hoped beyond hope he would still have the strength to use enough energy this far away from his home. But it was the only plan we had. I gave him a silent nod before moving closer.

I thanked the recent storms for making the forest floor wet so no dry twigs snapped under my feet. Still, I chose my path carefully.

"Again? What happened last time?" Penny asked. As if she anticipated an angry outburst from Liv, she pointed to the screen and added, "See that bar? It's going to take me a while. You might as well tell me while we wait."

Liv let out a frustrated snarl, but then said, "Courtney and I were best friends, until we weren't. I'm sure from reading your story, you know what I mean." Her tone was acidic, so much so I worried it might burn me merely by listening. "I'd joked with her about how my little brother was obsessed with her," she continued, softening a little. "You know, older sister stuff. I *never* thought she would repeat any of it. But we grew apart—well, more like Courtney dumped me for someone new—and a few months later, some guy was getting aggressive with her in the parking lot after a football game. Van was walking by, and he saved her, punching the guy in the face before pulling her away.

"When the police and her parents came to pick her up, she was telling them how Van was her savior. But the very next day a rumor started online that the only reason Van was there in the first place was because he was stalking Courtney and that he was the one she really needed to worry about. It ruined Van. Kids can be so mean and they took that and ran with it. He even dropped out when the depression kicked in. Our mom hired tutors to homeschool him for the rest of high school. To this day, he is adamant it wasn't Courtney who started the rumor, but I knew her too well." Liv cleared her throat. "It was part of the inside joke we had about him always being around when she was. When the stalking rumors started to circulate, I knew it had to be her."

There was a silence. I stopped, reaching out to a nearby tree to steady me as I held my breath. I was within a couple yards of them now.

"Is it done yet?" Liv snapped. She pointed the gun with renewed intensity as she looked over Penny's shoulder.

"Sorry, the internet is really slow out here." Penny's voice cracked with stress as she must've felt her time coming to an end. "You know, Courtney bullied me too. I hated her too. You don't have to do this. I won't say anything. I promise."

Liv snorted. "Sure, I believe you. And the moment you can get yourself protected, you'll write another tell-all piece about it. I know you think you're different from Courtney, but you're the same. You're both liars."

Checking on me one last time, SJ moved next to Liv, so he stood right in front of Penny. SJ watched Liv's hands like a dog begging for food. He was poised, knees bent, but didn't make a move. He motioned for me to raise the shovel. As I moved it above my head, panic filled my thoughts.

What if SJ couldn't push the gun far enough away from her? Would she run after it? Or follow us? My fingers clenched around the wooden shovel handle as I eyeballed the area I was aiming for.

As if she wanted to get the full story if she was going to die anyway, Penny said, "So you killed her ten years later for starting a rumor about your brother?"

"Of course not," Liv answered. "A friend of mine followed her on Instagram as Clover. We recognized her immediately, and when I read the part about Van proposing and her using it for entertainment value, I confronted her. I told her to give the ring back and take down the post. When she refused, things got a little heated. I didn't mean to kill her." I could hear the regret coating Liv's words at that confession.

"Now!" SJ called.

I channeled all of my fear and energy, I pulled my arms back then flung them forward. The shovel flew through the air past Liv and into the woods to her right. She jumped in surprise just as SJ hit her with a wave of energy. I waited until the gun left her hand and disappeared into a nearby shrub. Then I raced forward.

Penny stood there stunned, still clutching her phone. I reached for her arm and yanked her toward me. Her wild eyes widened as my presence registered in her brain.

Unfortunately, my presence also registered with Liv, who turned from where her gun had fallen. Anger burned in her eyes as she hesitated, her body moving toward the gun before she seemed to change her mind and come after us.

We weren't going to make it. *Could the two of us fight her off?* I wondered. *Maybe now that she didn't have the gun.*

But just as I was contemplating my lack of hand-to-hand combat skills, Liv stopped mid lunge. She slammed back as if having run into an invisible wall and fell to the ground.

"I'll hold her as long as I can," SJ said, but his voice was already faint and his body fast disappearing.

I didn't hesitate a moment more. I yanked Penny behind me as we ran, full speed, back toward the yurts, and hopefully, toward the incoming police.

The sound of someone crashing through brush behind us sent me running faster. Penny kept pace, and I no longer needed to drag her.

But even as Asher, the open field, and the yurts came into view ahead, the sickening click of gun's safety echoed through the forest behind us. Liv had found her gun.

The fear written on Asher's face said it all as he rushed forward, putting himself in between Liv and us. But I knew his energy had limits and he wouldn't be able to hold her forever, just as SJ hadn't been able to. We'd be easy targets running across the lawn or hiding in a yurt.

I'm not sure if it was the word *hiding* that gave me the idea or if it was the familiar tree trunk that came into view right then. But instead of running for the open field, I jumped to the right, pulling Penny with me.

"Trust me," was all I had time to whisper.

Without sparing another sound, I guided her around Asher's special hollowed tree trunk with me, disappearing into the secret entrance.

We crouched low in the space. It was tight with both of us in there. Sounds of a scuffle met our ears in faint bursts through the thick wood of the trunk. I strained to hear the sound of a gun clattering to the forest floor, proving Asher had gotten it away from her, but there was only silence.

Then Liv's footsteps squelched in the wet earth outside our hiding spot. She was breathing heavy like us. Penny and I held our breath as she approached, her steps slowing as she walked closer to the trunk.

Penny squeezed her eyes closed and I did the same.

And then the footsteps moved on. The sound of them disappearing into the distance had to be the greatest thing I'd ever experienced. Our eyes must've opened at the same moment. Penny's shoulders sagged in relief and we both leaned against the decaying interior walls of the hollowed trunk.

Until the footsteps returned, this time coming closer.

In the darkness, only the terrified whites of Penny's eyes stood out.

But all at once, there was the wet sound of tires crunching on the driveway on the road behind us. They were moving fast.

Asher appeared inside with us. "I should've figured you'd be in here," he said through a relieved sigh. "The police are here, but she's right outside. Stay quiet," Asher said in his faint voice. I could barely see the outline of him in the darkness of the trunk, and it took me a full second to realize he was gone a moment later.

The footsteps that had been near the trunk squelched away into the forest. More feet squished the soggy ground as people approached, these people obviously didn't care about being quiet. Someone took off at a run.

"Stop!" Clemenson's deep voice growled. But by the way the group thundered past us, I doubted that Liv listened.

Asher was back a minute later, a huge smile on his face. "They've got her. You're okay to come out," Asher said.

Relief wrapped around me, enveloping me in a way that released all the tension from my body. I almost toppled over from the suddenness of it all.

I put my finger to my lips and motioned to Penny that we should check outside. I led the way. Just as we emerged, the chief and Officers Kennedy and Girard walked up, leading a handcuffed Liv in front of them. Officer Girard's uniform was covered in mud on one side as if she'd tackled Liv to the ground. Judging by the mud covering the front of Liv, I'd say that was exactly what had happened. I reminded myself to give Officer Girard a free pastry next time she came into the tea shop, and also to never mess with her.

I waved to the group as Penny and I stood up straight.

The chief's face was full of relief in a way I'd never seen when he looked at me. Having not seen either of us around, he'd probably worried Liv had shot us both already.

"We're okay," I called.

Liv scowled at me as Officer Girard led her past us. "I'm going to take this one to the car, Chief," Girard said.

The chief nodded and instructed Kennedy to ride with her. He would meet them down at the station. "I'll be catching a ride with Miss Woodmere here." The way he said it made me sure I wasn't completely out of trouble. "Follow me, you two." He crooked a finger toward the house.

Rain was starting to fall again, and after the chilling experience we'd been through, I was looking forward to getting out of the cold. He left me standing at the other end of the covered porch as he talked to Penny first.

SJ appeared before me. "Your friend wanted me to tell you he'd see you back at the house," the ghost said, transparent and a little laggy even though we were standing on his porch. "He's going to go recover from the energy loss."

I turned my back toward the chief and Meadow. "Thank you so much," I whispered so they wouldn't hear. "I'm so glad you were here."

But as I met his gaze, the sadness in the ghost's features hit me in the gut like a flying shovel. While his grandson hadn't turned out to be a murderer, his granddaughter had.

"I'm so sorry about Liv, though."

He dipped his head in acceptance. "She made her choices. Just like my son. And now Van will carry on the Mills family name in peace and hopefully prosperity. Helping stop her from taking another life feels wonderful, however. I feel lighter somehow."

About to comment that it was probably from the energy loss, I realized he actually did appear lighter than he had a moment before. But he wasn't using energy right now. Which meant …

A smile curled across my face. "I think that was your unfinished business, SJ. I think you get to move on now."

A look of pure joy filled his face as he began to disintegrate. "I'll be sure to tell Richard what a lovely great-granddaughter he has." And with that, he was gone.

I sighed happily until Chief Clemenson approached me from behind and said, "Okay, Miss Woodmere. Care to explain what happened here?"

I decided to start with the truth—well, mostly the truth.

23

The hour the chief held me gave Asher time to recover, so he was back to normal once I returned. I was surprised by his quick recovery, but he explained all about how he'd been able to knock the gun from Liv's hands with a burst of energy. Then he'd gone in search of me and Penny. By the time he found us, the police were there and he hadn't needed to use any more energy.

We debriefed while I made myself dinner. The sun had just set and my stomach growled in protest. After my chilly evening, I wanted nothing more than comfort food, so I started some macaroni and cheese on the stove.

I was explaining to Asher the finer points of boxed macaroni and cheese when there was a knock on my front door. Pausing, I went to answer it, Asher by my side. On the other side of the glass were Daphne, Jolene, and Carl. They burst in when I opened the door.

"I've been calling you for half an hour, lady," Jolene said, holding up a bottle of wine.

My face heated as I remembered my phone on the passenger seat of my car, flying off into the footwell when

I'd taken that corner abruptly. I was so tired by the time I got home, I didn't even think to grab it.

"Rosie, you're a downright celebrity." Daphne said, planting a kiss on my cheek as she shoved past me. She held a casserole dish with two hands and it wafted scents of cheese and potatoes—and was that bacon too?—as she walked past.

I blinked. "What?"

Carl, the only one left outside—and looking wholly uncomfortable entering through the front door instead of via the porch like usual—grunted. "I don't know. They yammered about some kind of cheepers social media face tube." He swatted a calloused hand in my direction as he stepped inside, one arm wrapped around a large salad bowl.

Cheepers? I wondered as I closed the door behind them. Asher shrugged. I felt bad that our night alone was suddenly invaded, but Asher seemed delighted by the company and gestured for me to follow them.

By the time I reached the kitchen—I followed the noise—Daphne had her dish uncovered and sitting on the counter. I instantly recognized it as her famous twice-baked potato casserole and my stomach growled in anticipation. Sticking a serving spoon into the hot dish, she moved to the stove to finish my macaroni and cheese. Jolene had a bottle of wine open, and Carl took the foil off his bowl to reveal a delicious-looking salad underneath.

"You didn't have to do this," I said, shaking my head.

They all stared at me like I was crazy.

"We won't let you sit in this house alone after a day like that." Jolene waved the wine cork at me as she pulled it off the opener.

Asher and I sent each other a knowing glance and smiled.

Keeping my smile in place, I sat down at my kitchen table as Carl set a plate of casserole and salad in front of me. Jolene followed closely behind with a glass of wine.

After I'd taken my first few glorious bites, I said, "Okay, tell me how I'm internet famous." I guessed that's what Carl was referring to with all the random social media nouns he'd spouted before.

"That Penny Meadows girl tweeted about the whole experience," Jolene explained, being the one most familiar with the lingo out of the three.

I cocked an eyebrow, wondering if she'd actually been tweeting for help instead of deleting the post like Liv wanted. "What did she tweet?" I asked.

Carl huffed as if me using that word as a verb upset him.

Daphne chimed in from over by the stove. "A bunch of near death stuff to push people to her blog. She wrote a whole new blog post about the 'mystery girl' who saved her." Daphne turned off the burner and stirred the macaroni once more before saying, "Do you have a container I can put this in? There's no reason for you to have to eat this now. We have a real dinner." She wrinkled her nose at my from-a-box dinner.

Which meant … "So the chief really *did* listen to my hunch? My call was what got him up there?" I got up to fetch a container so I could save the macaroni for later.

Carl shook his head. "Apparently the brother cracked. Said he'd been afraid from the start that it had been his sister."

Jolene added, "That night, Liv was there because she'd driven in from the city to try to convince Van to kick Clover out of the commune. That, plus Liv and Clover's history together, made Van suspicious their decade-long fight had finally come to a violent end."

"So that's why Van lied and pretended not to know Clover," I said, remembering how he wanted to be the one to come to his sister's rescue for once.

"The boy's in a lick of trouble himself for trying to cover up a murder, but he came clean when it became clear it really had been his sister who murdered the girl," Carl said.

I snorted. "And here I'd been thinking it was my call that got the chief up there. I should've known. I guess he would've gotten there without me."

Everyone laughed.

"He might have, but they would've been too late to help that Penny girl. You're the only reason she's still alive," Daphne said pointedly.

Well, not just me. SJ and Asher were the real heroes. "Speaking of Penny, did she really call me, 'mystery girl'?" I asked, circling back.

Jolene chuckled. "Yep."

I think I surprised everyone when I let out a frustrated sigh. "I've met her so many times. And I saved her life. She can't even remember my name?"

Carl grumbled his matched disapproval.

"So I'm some sort of anonymous famous." I tipped my head to one side. "That doesn't sound so bad."

We chatted and laughed for a few hours until the bottle of wine was gone and we'd made a large dent in both Carl's salad and Daphne's casserole. And even though it was late when they left, I felt rejuvenated by their company so I popped out to my car to grab my phone and the hatbox of Abigail's letters.

Asher, who had seemed to thoroughly enjoy the company tonight, had also adopted a sad expression a few times when I could tell he wanted to say something or join in on the conversation and couldn't.

Standing in the tearoom once I was back inside, I proffered the box toward Asher. "In all the melee, I forgot to mention this," I said, pulling the dusty top off the box.

Asher leaned forward, glancing inside. The smell of dust and paper wafted up to greet us. Letters in bundles tied with yellowed ribbon took up most of the space in the box.

I chose one stack of letters at random, glancing at the addresses on the front. They were all to Abigail Glaser, of course, but it was the return address that caught my eye.

"From Mr. Asher Benson," I read aloud.

My eyes flashed up to meet Asher's. On closer examination, each stack started with a letter from Asher. There had to be fifty letters in the box, tied into stacks of ten.

"She kept the letters you wrote," I said.

Happiness tumbled through me at the thought. Maybe Abigail wasn't as terrible as I made her out to be. Maybe she did love Asher after all.

His face was a mask that held as much surprise as I'm sure mine did, but far more emotion. "She kept them?" he whispered.

A smile broke through my surprise and I set them aside. They wouldn't hold any clues we needed.

The realization that might not be true, hit me all at once. "Actually …" I said to myself as I thought. Seeing Asher was confused—proof he couldn't actually read my mind—I added, "Oh, I thought these wouldn't give us any clue as to why Sully would've killed you, but what if their existence is a clue?"

Asher's forehead wrinkled in question.

"If Sully found out she still loved you, Ash, he might have killed you to get you out of the picture."

Asher nodded, the gesture deepening the longer he did it. This was what he'd been waiting for, proof his nemesis had been his murderer, and yet he seemed like he couldn't quite believe it.

I remember experiencing a very similar emotional paradox when we found out the treatments had been successful and my leukemia was gone. I'd been looking forward to being in remission—it was all the doctors and my mother talked about as if saying it would make it true—and then when it came, I didn't know how to feel.

Placing my hand over—or through—Asher's ghostly one, where it rested on the side of the box, I said, "He must've found the letters, confronted her about them, and then flown off the handle."

"Or maybe he didn't even confront her," Asher offered. "It's possible she didn't know he found our letters, that he did all of that in secret so she thought I deserted." Asher's voice broke a little as he worked it out.

"Which meant she would see him as her best option since you were out of the picture." I nodded.

My delight waned as I realized what this meant. We had reasonable proof that Sully was the one to murder Asher. Between Asher's body being found on his property, to Abigail's worrisome last line of her journal, to now this: proof she still loved Asher and would've married him. This was the evidence we'd been searching for, the last bit that proved how Asher died.

This meant his unfinished business was officially resolved. Nothing held him back from moving on now. Based on the equally excited and devastated expressions that swept over Asher's face in the following moments, he realized this at the same time I did.

For something as wonderful as a spirit moving on, it was so awfully abrupt. When my grandmother's spirit moved on, I hadn't even realized that was what was happening. And then she was gone. SJ's departure had been just as quick. That meant we didn't have much time.

We blurted out at the same time.

"Ash, I can't tell you—"

"Rosie, your friendship has been—"

Stopping, we laughed. Tears gathered in the corners of our eyes.

Asher's mouth pulled into a bittersweet smile. "Let's not ruin this with trying to figure out the right things to say. We know what this has meant to both of us."

Tears streamed down my face now, and my lips trembled as I held back the worst of the sobs. I tried to smile. My body felt torn between two opposing emotions.

"Can I try something?" he asked, opening his arms.

My head jutted back. "Ash, we've tried hugging before," I said through a sniffle.

"Yes, but I've been working on something and I want to test it."

Wary but hopeful, I stepped forward with my arms opened wide as well. The last time we tried this, I'd passed right through him. I closed my eyes as I had during our first trial.

But this time, my body stopped when it hit something solid. Arms closed around me. Eyes flying open, I gasped.

"How are you doing this?" I squeezed my arms around him.

Asher beamed. "I've been practicing with the coat rack at night, when you're asleep. I have to focus my energy outward, all over instead of just at one object." As he spoke, his voice grew faint and his body dimmed.

It was happening. He was leaving me.

I must've been leaning into him too much, because I fell

forward, straight through to the other side of his body as the energy became too much for him to sustain.

I spun around, not wanting to miss a moment. He did too, his eyes full of love and sadness. After a few seconds, I waved to give my brain something else to focus on other than the tears I felt building.

When I was still waving seconds later, a confusion tugged the corners of my mouth down.

"Is this not it?" I whispered.

Asher frowned, his movements delayed. When he spoke it was listing and distant. "I don't know. I thought something was happening, but maybe it's all the energy I used to hug you."

That made sense. The hard thing was that the disappearance that happened when ghosts used intense amounts of energy looked very similar to the vanishing they did as they moved on.

I pressed my lips together for a moment. "SJ's unfinished business wasn't about his death, rather him helping us save a life today. Maybe you're here for a different reason than figuring out who killed you. It could be to help prevent me from doing something stupid." I chanced a smile, hoping to lighten the mood but not wishing to be insensitive to what Asher was going through.

He nodded slowly as he thought—or he could've been nodding at regular speed, but it was made sluggish by his reduced energy. "True. I don't feel anything different. You said SJ felt lighter … ready, right?"

I confirmed that.

"I don't feel ready," he said.

We stood there for a moment. I couldn't speak for Asher, but I didn't know what to say or do at that point. It felt wrong to celebrate. My tears had dried up, at least.

From the exhale he let out and the slight smile tugging up the corners of his mouth, Asher didn't seem heartbroken either. In fact, he almost looked relieved. And even though he'd been waiting a century to cross over, maybe he didn't mind waiting a little longer.

"Shall we do some reading?" I suggested.

"That sounds lovely, Rosemary," Asher said, then let me lead the way into the library.

24

A full week later and Asher was still with me. We'd stayed up late that night, waiting and wondering if he would move on at any moment. Even though we'd planned on reading, we spent the time talking until I couldn't keep my eyes open any longer.

Waking up the next morning to Asher reading a newspaper in the tearoom filled me with equal parts relief and worry. That morning, we devised a plan to help as many people—living and not—to fulfill whatever unfinished business he had. If it wasn't the mystery of his murder keeping him here, it must be that.

Today, however, we were focused on books. It was our monthly book club meeting. The chatter in the tearoom was all similar iterations of the same sentiment: they didn't think they would enjoy reading a children's book, but they had. Quite a lot, actually, I gathered from listening to them chat over their refreshments as we waited for everyone to show up.

Mom had come down on Friday and spent most of the

day in bed, recovering from the library's fundraising extravaganza. But with a couple cups of coffee and the promise of literary conversations—her greatest energy source—she was smiling and ready to get started.

We had a rousing discussion of the book, and unlike normal, Mom drove home that evening instead of staying the whole weekend. She was still beat from her overtime and had neglected some work at her place that she wanted to finish on Sunday.

As it turned out, it was good Mom left early.

Just before dinner, I caught sight of the hatbox of Abigail's letters sitting on the corner of the coffee table in the library.

"Ash," I called out, having seen him in the tearoom. "Do you want me to hold on to these letters or should I return them to The Pines?" I asked when he appeared in the room next to me.

He contemplated that for a moment. "I think I'm okay letting them go. I remember writing them like it was yesterday, and the ones she wrote to me are what really count. Those are lost forever, I think. Let Van have these. He needs all the positive family news he can get lately."

I agreed. News around town was that Van was officially staying at The Pines, for good. The chief had dropped the obstruction charges against him since he'd finally come clean and no one else had been hurt. Van had been so touched by his community members coming to his support that day the chief brought him in for questioning, that he said he felt like they were his new family.

When I'd heard that, I knew SJ would've been proud of Van for making his own family.

And even though Liv had been trying to protect her little brother—and swore she hadn't meant to kill Clover—she wouldn't be spending time with Van soon. Between second-degree murder charges and attempted murder, things weren't looking promising for her upcoming trial.

Agreeing with Asher's final decision about the letters, I grabbed the bundle we'd brought out and stuffed it back into the box. But before I replaced the lid, something caught my eye.

It had probably been undetectable whenever Abigail had put the letters into this box, but time and the elements had warped the false bottom, leaving a gap.

There was something else below the letters. Asher must've spotted it too. He leaned in closer. His ghostly forehead almost passed through mine as I removed the bundles of letters. Once those were gone, the false bottom was even more recognizable. I pinched one corner and pulled.

If it had once been glued into place, that glue had all decayed because it lifted out with little resistance.

Underneath it was another diary, almost identical to the one we'd read through before. Asher and I looked at each other for a breath before glancing back at the diary. With a nod from Asher, I extracted the thing and set the box aside.

I fell onto the couch as if my knees could no longer support me. Asher settled next to me. There wasn't any pomp and circumstance, or even much hesitation when I opened the diary to the first page.

At that point, I didn't know what I held or what the pages would contain.

I didn't know I needed to be wary.

After confirming it was Abigail's journal by the name in the front and her handwriting, we started reading the first entry. It was dated only days after the last one we'd read in the last diary.

Dear Diary,

Sully and I had a terrible argument today. It was awful. We were discussing the 'Asher problem' as we've come to call it, and the man suggested the most ridiculous thing. His plan was that I push to marry Asher before he goes off to war so I can get his money and then hopefully he'll die on the battlefield and I'll be a war widow. He says the two of us can be together, and then we'd have all the money we've always deserved but never had.

I became so cross with him because what if Asher doesn't die in the war? Where would we be, then? Did he want to take that big of a risk with our lives, our love?

He became cross with my crossness, asking if I had a better plan.

Diary, I fear writing this down might be incriminating but I do have a better plan. I've thought of something terrible and devious. It's risky and could very well ruin me … but it might just work.

I wanted to throw the diary. I wanted to stomp on it and burn it. I also couldn't let it go. My pulse pounded in my ears as I held my quaking fingers above the page, unsure if I should turn it or rip it out.

"Ash, this …"

He cleared his throat. "This is proof Sully didn't kill me," he said flatly. "So that's why I didn't move on. We had it wrong." He closed his eyes. "So wrong."

I hated the part I'd played in getting his hopes up so much. I think I'd been almost as excited about the proof of Abigail's love for him as he had been.

"I'm so sorry. This is—" I tried again, but he interrupted me.

"Possibly proof Abigail was the one to kill me." He

exhaled, sitting back as if the words on the page were flames and they were growing much too hot for him to be so close to.

I swallowed my reservations before asking, "Do you want to keep reading? Maybe we're wrong. Maybe that line just sounded ominous and her plan was to elope with Sully." I let my eyebrows rise along with my tone, trying to be the voice of hope.

I tried not to let the fact that she'd obviously gone through the trouble to hide this diary destroy the insignificant amount of hope I was grasping at.

Asher watched the waves out the window as if they called to him. I almost repeated the question, wondering if he'd even heard me, when he shook his head.

"Rosie, do you mind if I don't read it?" His blue eyes met mine. "I know we said no secrets, but can I ask you to do this for me? Would you read through and tell me what you find?" he asked, amending that by saying, "No, I'm sorry. I can't do that to you. That's an awful position to put you in."

Setting my shoulders back, I pushed aside any reservations. "You don't have to ask me, I'm offering."

If Asher needed me to be that buffer, I would. If Asher needed me to be strong for him in this hard time, I could. I was Rosie. Because of Asher's friendship, encouragement, and love, I'd grown through the hardest parts of my life, and I wanted to be here for Asher's.

Like SJ and Great-Grandpa Richard, Ash and I were those kind of friends. We made each other better people.

I put my hand through Asher's. He looked down, smiled, and I felt his hand clasp over mine as he used energy like he had to hug me. He dimmed before taking his hand away.

Closing the diary, I put it aside. I would read it later,

when he wasn't sitting right next to me. And I would get to the bottom of this, once and for all.

My friend deserved that.

NEXT IN THE SERIES:

Follow Rosemary and Asher as their story continues in the next installment of the Pebble Cove Teahouse Mysteries …

Get your copy today!

Pebble Cove is known for giving tourists the cold shoulder, but a frozen body is something new.

The people of Pebble Cove are thrown into a forced hibernation when the worst snow storm in a decade hits the Oregon Coast. They expect to find damages once the snow thaws, but a frozen body down by the pier comes as a terrible surprise.

Rosemary is keeping warm with an abundance of chai tea, wooly sweaters, and further research into Asher's past. But when a second body is found, she can't deny the chilling thoughts that the two deaths might be connected. Or that this might not be the end.

ALSO BY ERYN SCOTT

Mystery:

The Pepper Brooks Cozy Mystery Series

The Stoneybrook Mysteries

Pebble Cove Teahouse Mysteries

Women's fiction:

The Beauty of Perhaps

Settling Up

The What's in a Name Series

In Her Way

I Pick You

Romantic comedy:

Meet Me in the Middle

ABOUT THE AUTHOR

Eryn Scott lives in the Pacific Northwest with her husband, two cats, and a dog. She loves classic literature, musicals, knitting, and hiking. She writes cozy mysteries and women's fiction.

Join her newsletter to learn about new releases and sales!

www.erynscott.com

Made in United States
North Haven, CT
17 April 2022

18351715R00125